DEADLY DECEPTION

OLD CITY MYSTERIES: BOOK ONE

RAINY KIRKLAND

RAINYKIRKLAND.COM

To Andy and Hank -
who could not stay to hear the tale.
Love and miss you both.

CHAPTER 1

Late January 1880 - Tocoi, Florida

*S*ecret Service Agent Andrew Langley stared at the postmaster in disbelief. "What do you mean the railroad won't run again until Friday? I need to get to St. Augustine now."

"Then you'd be wanting to take the stagecoach," the postmaster suggested, mopping the sweat from his face with a handkerchief that once might have been white. "'Cept, he's already left for today's run. He'll be back tomorrow then will run again the next day."

Andrew stepped away from the counter. He'd been in Atlanta for more than a month successfully dismantling a counterfeiting ring, but now his entire focus was to get back to St. Augustine as quickly as possible. Clarissa, the love of his life, had finally agreed to marry him, and the engagement ring he'd purchased while working in Atlanta was burning a hole in his pocket.

Andrew decided that since the usual transportation wasn't available, he would simply take matters into his own hands and find a private carriage for the last four-hour leg of his trip. Turning, he found himself facing a stranger dressed almost as finely as himself.

"Sir?"

"Yes…?"

"Allow me to introduce myself. I'm Samuel Thompson, originally from Philadelphia. I couldn't help but overhear that you need to get to St. Augustine, as do I. And since I don't relish waiting another few days for the railway, I was contemplating renting a private coach for the journey. I'd just finished inquiring when I overheard you speaking with the postmaster. Would you be interested in sharing a coach with me?"

Andrew felt his mood lighten. "It was my good fortune to bump into you today, Mr. Thompson. Let's get this venture underway."

Soon they were seated facing each other in a covered carriage and on their way.

"Are you traveling to St Augustine on business?" Thompson asked as the carriage rocked and swayed.

"No, but I often visit." Andrew smiled and pulled a small photograph from the inside pocket of his coat. "I plan to be married soon. This is my Clarissa," he said with pride as he extended the photo.

Thompson accepted the tintype and smiled in appreciation. "She is a beauty." He handed the photo back. "Since you are well versed about our destination, might you recommend a good hotel where one may reside while on business?"

"The Magnolia and the Hernandez Hotels are both quite adequate. What is your business?" Andrew took one last look at the photo before returning it to his pocket.

"My company imports textiles and trims from England and France. As you know, the ladies are always after the latest fashions and we try to accommodate. So which of those two hotels would you recommend?"

Andrew smiled thinking of Clarissa and how she poured over every copy of her women's magazines, looking for illustrations of Worth's latest designs from Paris. "Do you carry letters of personal reference?"

Thompson nodded and patted his breast pocket. "Of course."

"Then I would recommend a boarding house for your visit, rather than a hotel. You'll want the Wakefield House on Charlotte Street. Best food in the city. If you wish, I'll introduce you to Mrs. Wakefield when we arrive as I am currently staying there myself."

"That would be most appreciated." Thompson pulled a deck of cards from his pocket. "Would you fancy a game or two to help pass the time?"

Andrew grinned. "What's your pleasure?" His grin grew even wider as he won the first hand and then the second. "We should have put a dollar or two on the hand," he said as the deck was passed to him to deal.

"You'd like to place a bet?"

Andrew shrugged. "Why not? Add a little excitement to the game."

Thompson hesitated for a moment. "Well if you insist, I guess I could afford to lose a dollar or two. After all, if business in the city goes as well as I hope, a dollar here or there won't break the bank. Deal away, good sir."

Andrew won the next two hands. As the deck was passed back to Thompson for the deal, the coach hit a particularly bumpy patch of road. Looking out the window, Andrew watched an alligator slither back into the swampy water that edged one side of the road. He removed his coat in concession to the heat and proceeded to win the next four hands.

"You're too good for me, sir," Thompson said wearily.

"You want to stop?"

"I fear you're going to clean me out if I don't."

"As you wish," Andrew said, raising his arms for a stretch. Suddenly he felt a pain, a stabbing agony. He looked down to see a blade sticking out of his chest. Confused, he looked up at Thompson. "What…"

"No one interferes with my business and lives to tell about it." Thompson reached over and gave the knife an upward jerk. Andrew managed a single gasp before his heart stopped.

Withdrawing the knife, Thompson carefully cleaned the blade. Then, mindful of the blood, he removed Andrew's ring, pocket watch, and wallet. But his breath caught when he located the badge that identified Andrew Langley as a Secret Service Agent. He knew from his informants that Langley had been the one to bring about the demise of his very profitable counterfeit ring in Atlanta, but his information had not included the fact that the man was indeed an agent.

Thompson replayed in his mind their recent conversations. It was clear that Langley hadn't known he had been involved with the ring or the man wouldn't have offered to take him to the very boarding house where he himself lived. Or would he? Thompson paused. Had that been offered as a way to keep abreast of his activities? No, Langley wasn't that clever, he decided. Methodically he went through Langley's bag then quickly transferred everything of value to his own valise. Delighted when he found another bundle of cash, he tucked some in his own pockets before securing the rest in his bag. He stared for a long moment at the photo Andrew had shown him. Yes, he thought, she would do very nicely. The last thing he did before banging on the ceiling to alert the driver was to tuck the photo and the velvet box with Clarissa's ring into his coat pocket.

The carriage pulled to a stop and Thompson leaned out the window. "Mr. Langley is feeling poorly. He needs to step out for a moment or two."

The driver gave a nervous glance around at the thick vegetation that lined the narrow roadway. "We'd best not be stopping long," he said anxiously. "The Indians ain't been trouble for a while now but I don't want to be no sitting target, if you get my meaning."

"It won't take but a moment," Thompson assured. "Come give me a hand helping Mr. Langley."

"So ya done it then?" the driver asked as he climbed down from his perch and looked into the carriage at the body.

"No one disrupts one of my operations and walks away. But why wasn't I informed that he was an agent?"

The man's eyes widened as he turned back to Thompson. "He's an agent? Ya killed an agent?"

"He carries a badge," Thomson said, pulling on his gloves.

"Wait, when ya asked me to help ya with this job ya never said nothing about him being an agent and all. This is gonna come down hard if folks was to find out. Them agents don't take kindly to one of their own being killed."

"Then no one better find out, my fine fellow," Thompson said, reaching into the carriage to grab Langley's feet. "Now get in there and get his shoulders before he bleeds all over the carriage."

"But…"

"Look, I'm the one who made the arrangements. You're the only one who knows that this fool chose to join me. So stop worrying and help me carry him."

Wary of snakes, they stepped quickly through the under-brush and dropped Andrew in a heap behind a clump of palmetto trees.

"That should do it," Thompson said when they were back at the coach. "It won't take long for the gators to find him." He pulled a wad of cash from his pocket. "Here is your fee."

Licking his lips at the offered cash, the driver nodded quickly. "You'll be in touch when ya get things up and running again?"

Thompson climbed back into the carriage. "I know how to find you. Now drive on and see if you can make up the time we lost here."

∼

EMMA WAKEFIELD CLOSED her ledger with a satisfied smile. Despite the fact that she had three empty rooms, her bank balance was steadily growing. Returning the ledger to its cubby on her desk, she picked up the photo of her husband. "I think you'd be proud of me," she whispered, fighting back a sudden rush of tears. James had been gone for just over a year and his image still tugged at her heart.

"One more business trip," he had promised. "I'll make this run to New York, check on my parents, and then be home for good and we can start our family."

She'd stood on the dock and waved goodbye until he was out of sight. Weeks later, she received news of the flu outbreak. Before she could make arrangements to travel, the dreaded telegram arrived. James and his parents were gone, leaving her and James's elderly Aunt Daisy as the only surviving family members. She'd cried for days wishing only to join James in the afterlife. But eventually Emma realized she had to face her situation head on.

James had left some money, enough that she could live in comfort for a number of years. But there was Aunt Daisy to think of. Considering remarriage was out of the question, so acting against the advice of many, she'd taken a goodly portion of her inheritance and painstakingly converted the unusual L shaped Wakefield family home into the Wakefield Boarding House. The ground floor was now comprised of a public parlor, dining room, and six bedrooms, each with access to the open porch. The second floor provided Emma with her own set of private rooms, a place for Aunt Daisy, and six more bedrooms, each opening onto the balcony. The third floor attic was fitted for the servants. She could accommodate up to twenty guests at a time, and thanks to Sadie's outstanding cooking and her own hostessing abilities, Wakefield House's reputation was starting to grow.

"The holidays were so hard without you," she whispered, letting her fingers trace over his image. "Christmas, New Year's Eve..." She took a deep breath and straightened in her chair. "I know there are still empty rooms, but we're going to make it. It's a new year and I have every confidence it's going to be a good one. The fig trees you planted still thrive and seven orange trees survived the last freeze and are still bearing fruit. I just wish you were still here to see them." Reluctantly she returned the photo to its place of honor on her desk.

She heard footsteps on the balcony moments before a sharp knock and the door to her office flew open. Aunt Daisy rushed in with arms aflutter. "There's a gentleman downstairs asking for accommodations," she gasped.

"Come sit," Emma guided the elderly woman into a chair, "and calm yourself. Do you want some water?"

Daisy waved her away. "I was about to leave for the post office when he showed up at the door."

Emma smiled. "That's wonderful news. You know we still have empty rooms. Did he mention a length of stay?"

"I didn't ask because I don't like him."

"Why? What's wrong with him?"

"He makes me shiver," she huffed. "And I don't like him. He shouldn't stay here."

"You didn't send him away, did you?" Emma asked with alarm.

Her wits gathered, Daisy rose and straightened her hat. "I left that for you to do," she said firmly. "He's waiting with Gibbs in the main parlor. Now, I've delayed long enough. I'm off to the post office to see who the stagecoach brings in and get the newest copy of the *Gazette*. She rose and walked primly to the door. "Send him on his way, Emma dear. Just send him on his way. Oh, and Mrs. Milksop said to be sure to tell you that the tea was much too hot at dinner today." And with that declaration Aunt Daisy departed.

Dear dear Mrs. Milksop, Emma thought, closing the door to her office and making her way down the stairs. The tea was always too hot or too cold, the biscuits too flaky or not flaky enough.

Agatha and Wallace Milksop had traveled from Connecticut to find warmer weather for Mrs. Milksop's health and thus signed on for the remainder of the season. But their complaints would have to wait until she had dealt with the gentleman in the parlor.

Emma took a moment to tuck a stray curl back under her cap. Unless he looks like a common thug, she thought, I'll not be sending anyone away when we have empty rooms. Stepping into the parlor, she smiled at their ancient butler, Gibbs. He'd been a fixture in the Wakefield family for longer than even Aunt Daisy could remember. His body had grown frail, but his posture remained ramrod straight as he turned and greeted Emma.

"Mrs. Wakefield," his tone formal, "I'd like to introduce Mr. Samuel Thompson who has come seeking lodging."

"Thank you, Gibbs. Would you check on Sadie and see how she's proceeding with the evening meal?"

"As you wish, Madam."

Emma turned to their visitor and understood why he

made Aunt Daisy shiver. He was incredibly handsome with a firm chin and a tidy mustache and clothes that clearly pegged him as an upper class gentleman. "Mr. Thompson," she nodded her head slightly, "what brings you to St. Augustine?"

"I'm here on business," he said. "And I must say it's a pleasure to meet you. I've heard nothing but wonderful comments about Wakefield House."

Emma put on her most business-like smile. "And do you carry any letters of reference?"

Samuel reached into his inside jacket pocket and withdrew an envelope. "I hope these might suffice."

Taking the envelope, Emma quickly scanned the contents. "You have impressive letters of introduction from Mayor Wheaton of Savannah and Mayor Courtenay from Charleston."

Of course they're impressive, Samuel thought. I wrote them myself.

"But I see the seals are missing on both."

Samuel winced. "I've been traveling for the past few months on business and I fear with the heavy humidity the wax seals came undone sometime back." He began to search his pockets. "I believe I still carry one if you'd give me a moment to locate it."

"That won't be necessary," Emma smiled, handing back the documents. "I can see the wax stain on the letters and last summer was particularly steamy."

"Thank you for understanding," he said, tucking the letters back in his coat pocket.

"You said you'd been traveling. May I inquire as to the nature of your business?"

"I'm in import-export," Samuel said, taking in the quality of the furniture that filled the room. "My company imports textiles and trims from both England and France."

"How interesting that must be, Mr. Thompson. Here in

St. Augustine we are so fortunate to have access to nearly everything one could want and it's due to businessmen like yourself bringing trade to our fair city. How did you hear of Wakefield House?"

"You honor me, Mrs. Wakefield." Samuel gave a slight bow. "An old friend said should I ever find myself in St. Augustine, I must stay at Wakefield House. He was quite emphatic about it." When Emma remained silent he continued. "His name is Langley, and I was led to believe he stayed here often."

"Would that be Andrew Langley?"

Samuel smiled again. "Exactly, then you do know him. Mr. Langley and I shared a number of meals while we each finalized our business arrangements in Atlanta. That's when he insisted that should I ever travel this far south, I owed it to myself to stay here." He looked about the well-appointed parlor. "And I can certainly see why."

With the mention of Andrew's name, Emma let her body relax. "Mr. Langley is often a resident. And his recommendation is much appreciated. Do you have a length of stay in mind, sir?"

Samuel shifted his hat from one hand to the other. "I'm not sure at this moment, but I'm thinking at least a month to start, with the possibility of continuing through the rest of the season."

"Then we can accommodate you," Emma said. "Our fee is two dollars a day but there is a discount if you book monthly."

"Monthly will do." Samuel pulled out his wallet exposing a large wad of cash. "I'll pay for a month in advance and then we'll see how it goes."

Emma accepted the money, slipping it deep into the pocket of her apron. "Then if you'll follow me, sir, I'll show you to your room. I'm afraid you've missed dinner today, but we will be serving supper at six. The evening fare is a selection of cold meats, bread, and, if I'm not mistaken, Sadie, our cook, is preparing a delicious fish stew to complete the meal. There will be sweets and Sadie's ginger cake is not to be missed. Coffee and tea will be available, as well as a light claret. Should you wish something stronger, please feel free to bring your own selection. If you place it on the sideboard Gibbs will gladly pour it for you."

Leading the way from the lobby to the open porch Emma continued. "Breakfast is available at six for the early risers, then again at eight for those who choose a later start to their day. Once you decide which time suits your schedule just advise Gibbs and your place will be set." She stopped in front of a door and taking a key from the ring that hung at her waist, opened it, stepping back so Thompson could enter first.

Like the parlor the room was airy and well appointed. A bed and night stand with lamp stood against one wall and a wardrobe and desk flanked a stone fireplace. A mirror hung over the wash stand and a colorful rug covered part of the wooden floor. "You'll probably not need the netting," Emma said, gesturing to the mosquito netting that hung from the ceiling over the bed. "The weather is most pleasant this time of year but the nights can become quite chilly. Henny will clean your room daily and lay kindling for a fire, so please feel free to advise her should a need arise."

Samuel wandered the room. Yes, this would do, and very nicely. "I can see why Mr. Langley was so complimentary, Mrs. Wakefield. The room is quite satisfactory."

"Then I'll leave you to get settled and…"

"Excuse me, madam," Gibbs said from the open doorway. "Forgive me for interrupting but Miss Clarissa has just arrived. Shall I escort her to your private parlor?"

"Thank you Gibbs, please do so." She turned back to

Thompson. "Do you have any questions, sir?" she asked moving to the doorway.

"No, thank you. Please feel free to attend to your guest."

With that Emma turned and started toward the stairs at the end of the porch. She never noticed Samuel Thompson stepping into the doorway behind her as he pulled a photo from his inside coat pocket. He watched the elderly butler assist a beautiful young woman from her carriage and his smile grew. Perfect, he thought. Everything was going to be just perfect.

CHAPTER 2

*E*mma greeted Clarissa with a hug. "You look radiant," she said leading the young woman to the sofa. "How are the wedding plans progressing?"

Clarissa beamed and her blond curls bounced. "I'm so excited. When Andrew returns from this trip we'll formally announce our engagement. My mother is over the moon and every day she has another idea for the engagement party. Her latest is that we should have a fountain that spouts champagne!"

"It sounds marvelous." Emma gave Clarissa's hand a squeeze. "Have you decided on your dress?"

"That's why I came." Clarissa pulled a folded illustration from her reticule. "I've finally made a decision." Carefully she smoothed the illustration. The dress pictured was the height of fashion in white satin with handmade lace on the bodice. The off-the-shoulder design was accented with additional lace and delicate satin bows holding tiny bouquets of baby roses.

"Oh my, that's gorgeous," Emma gasped. "You'll be the most beautiful bride."

"I've been doing my research," Clarissa declared, gazing lovingly at the illustration. She looked up. "I simply must convince Andrew that we should be married on a Wednesday. It will bring us luck you know," she said with conviction, refolding the paper and carefully placing it back in her bag.

"A Wednesday?" Emma struggled to keep the skepticism from her voice.

Clarissa nodded. "Didn't you read the *Cat's Meow* column in the *Gazette* last week? It clearly stated that Wednesday was the very best day for a wedding. I don't want to take the chance that we'll accidentally do something to bring misfortune."

Now Emma struggled to keep her smile in place. She knew all too well about bad luck and how even the best intentions could be ripped apart. "I'm going to miss you so much when you move. Here I finally get you married to my cousin and you're going to leave me."

"None of that," Clarissa said reaching for Emma's hand. "You'll have me tearing up and Savannah isn't that far away. But I must admit, every time I start thinking about running my own household my stomach starts to flutter. Of course then I think of all the decorating I can do and I'm all right again." She giggled. "It's such a grand house."

"I only visited once and that was years and years ago for an elderly uncle's birthday celebration, but I remember being very impressed. I'm so glad Andrew was able to purchase it for you."

"I'm jealous that you've actually been there but I've only seen photographs. But tell me…"

They were interrupted when Gibbs knocked gently on the door then entered pushing a cart with a silver tea service. A china plate held a collection of delicate pastries and confections.

"Oh, you didn't need to bother," Clarissa looked longingly at the choices. "I really shouldn't."

Emma thanked Gibbs and poured the tea, handing a cup to Clarissa. "I don't know what I'd do without Sadie. The woman is a marvel with sweets." She lifted the china plate and extended it to Clarissa. "We need to celebrate."

Clarissa selected a tiny cake topped with a dollop of cream. "I shouldn't, but these are too tempting." She took a delicate bite and sighed. "And so delicious."

The two women spent the next hour discussing and dissecting every aspect of the upcoming wedding until Clarissa glanced at the clock. "Oh my, I've overstayed my welcome." She stood quickly, trying to ignore the empty plate of treats.

"You're always welcome. And I love hearing all the details, but you're right, the hour has gotten away from us and I need to check the progress for our evening meal." As Emma rose, the door to the parlor edged slightly open.

"Oh my." Clarissa raised a hand to her lips as a sleek black cat marched proudly into the room. "What's that in his mouth?" she gasped. "Pray tell it's not a rat."

Emma stepped closer and sighed. Bending down she reached for the offering. "Come here Bandit, what have you pilfered this time?"

"You named your cat Bandit?"

"Not mine," Emma retrieved a man's sock and held it carefully by two fingers. "The Milksops brought him down with them from Connecticut. They're here for her health and insisted the cat stay with them."

"Oh my." Clarissa grinned.

"It wouldn't be a problem," Emma said as she walked over to the desk to drop the cat's offering. "Except Bandit has a talent for stealing. Heaven knows who this one belongs to.

I've had to instruct the guests to be sure their doors are closed tight but the little thief still manages to get in somehow."

Clarissa smothered a giggle. "Whatever will you do?"

Emma just shook her head. "I take them to the laundry and wait to find the mate," she said simply as the cat turned and strutted back out of the room.

⁓

EMMA KNEW she didn't need to check on the preparations for supper. Sadie was by far the best cook in town. But it had always been Emma's practice to see what was happening in the kitchen.

The kitchen, entirely separate from the house proper, was a single room. Walls lined with shelves held baskets, pots and utensils. One short wall held the bread oven and fireplace. In the center of the room stood a long wooden work table where a young boy sat with a bowl of soup and a meat sandwich. Seeing her the youngster sank into himself in an effort to disappear.

Sadie, who had been stirring a pot on the hearth, turned. "Good afternoon, Mrs. Wakefield. That there's Willie Jefferson. He's been helping me carry from the market. I hope you don't mind I gave him a bite."

"Not at all, Sadie." Emma smiled at Willie. "Pleased to meet you, young man."

Willie sprang to his feet and wiped his hand on his pants before extending it. "Yes, missus. Thank you, missus."

"How's the soup?"

"Oh, wonderful, missus. Best I ever had."

Observing his ill-fitting and threadbare clothes, Emma wondered if Willie ever had fish soup with actual fish in it.

"Good, I'm happy to hear that you approve. Please, sit down and finish it before it gets cold."

She turned to Sadie. "We will be having another guest at dinner."

"Yes, ma'am. Gibbs sent word."

Of course he did. There were times when Emma thought that Wakefield House could run perfectly well without her.

Out of the corner of her eye she saw Willie push one half of his sandwich into his front pocket. Was he saving it for later, she wondered, or did he have another soul he was needing to feed?

It was nearly dark when Willie peeked in through the dirt-encrusted window of the ground floor room he shared with his father. He always liked to see what was about to befall him before he entered. Tonight he was in luck. His old man appeared to be asleep on the ancient pallet which served as his bed. But as Willie quietly stepped in, he found that not to be the case.

"What are ya doin' being home so late?" Frank Jefferson bellowed, his British accent getting stronger the angrier he got.

Willie stopped in his tracks, setting his jaw against what was sure to come. "I brought you half a sandwich. It's a good one."

"Did ya now? And what d'ya think I'm to do with half a sandwich without a pint to go down with it?"

Willie took the sandwich from his pocket, blew the lint off it, and tentatively handed it to his father. "Take it 'round to the pub and get yourself a drink, then," he dared to say, stepping back quickly to be out of his father's reach.

"They don't give free drinks at McConnell's, ya daft lad, ya knows that."

"No work today then?" Willie sighed. From his right pocket he took a few coins. "Have today's earnings. It's all I got." He was lying about that. He'd been saving money for as long as he'd been earning it, one or two coins at a time, in a secret place down by the barracks. Someday, somehow, he would have enough to get out on his own.

To Willie's immense relief, his father took the coins and the sandwich and left. Willie crawled under the wide, heavy table that stood against the inside wall. That was where he slept, on the floor, out of reach of a father often too drunk to navigate across the room.

～

McCONNELL'S WAS busy on this Thursday night, filled with cigar smoke and the stench of unwashed bodies. Samuel Thompson pushed his way through the crowd to the bar where he managed to get a pint of lager and then he looked around for a likely target. He would need to find some patsies if his plans were to work. An unkempt man with a scraggly beard caught his eye. Thompson casually approached him, raising his glass in a silent salute. The man nodded, raising his nearly empty half pint as well.

"Can I get you another?" Samuel knew what the answer would be. Moments later, having secured a pitcher of lager, he was sitting at a table with a wide-eyed Frank Jefferson. He filled Frank's glass.

"You're local, I take it?" he asked.

"Aye, nowadays."

"Name's Thompson, Samuel Thompson."

"Frank Jefferson. Thanks for the drink."

"Lots of folks here tonight. Always this many?"

"Yup."

"Nothing else to do in St. Augustine?"

"Plenty to do. Depends on what ya likes."

Samuel nodded but fell silent for a while. Then he replenished the man's drink. "Perhaps, Mr. Jefferson, you might know of a place where a gentleman might have a bit of a wager?"

Frank looked at him skeptically. "If it's a bit of gamin' you're after there's always a few lads here on a Saturday night."

"And you sir?"

"Aye, I'm here most times." Frank stared into his glass a minute, then looked up. "Come by here at nine on Saturday and you can meet the chaps."

"I'll do that, Mr. Jefferson." Samuel raised his glass. "And thank you for it."

"Don't be thankin' me just yet," Jefferson chuckled. "We'll see if ya still have a shirt on your back come Sunday mornin.'"

EMMA STOOD on her balcony and breathed deeply. She loved afternoons like this. The weather was sunny and clear. She smiled as a carriage pulled to a halt in front of her walkway and she recognized Clarissa's driver. Making her way quickly down the steps, she took one look at her friend's face and knew something was amiss.

"Clarissa, good afternoon."

Clarissa struggled to smile in return. "I'm sorry to barge in on you this way." Then, glancing about, she added, "Might I speak with you inside?"

Emma extended her hand. "Of course. You must stay for tea. And Marcus," she looked up at the driver who was trying not to listen to their conversation, "if you were to pull the carriage around to the back and pay Sadie a visit in the kitchen, I'm sure she would offer you some of the molasses cookies she served at our noonday meal."

The driver tipped his hat and nodded. "Many thanks, Mrs. Wakefield, I'll do just that."

Emma was leading her guest into the front parlor when Gibbs appeared. "Might I assist you, madam?" he asked.

"Would you ask Sadie to prepare tea for my guest and advise her that I invited Marcus to stop by the kitchen while he waits."

"I'll see to it immediately." Then as quietly as he had arrived Gibbs was gone.

Emma led Clarissa to the sofa at the end of the room. "Now, tell me what has put you in such distress. Is something amiss with the wedding plans?"

Clarissa shook her head and began to wring the lace handkerchief she clutched. "I'm embarrassed to ask," she said slowly, her face awash in misery.

"My dear," Emma prompted gently, "you may ask me anything."

"Has Andrew returned?" Clarissa's words came out in a rush. "Is he in residence?"

Emma blinked in surprise. Whatever she'd imagined the problem to be it was certainly not this. "No, Andrew is working in Atlanta, you know that."

A tear traced down Clarissa's pale cheek quickly followed by another. "I don't know whether to be relieved or alarmed," she said quietly. "His last correspondence said he'd be returning on Wednesday but he wasn't on the stagecoach when it arrived. I had my maid wait to see if he came by private coach yesterday but he wasn't there either. Then today the railway came in and still no Andrew." At the knock at the door, she quickly averted her face and brushed at her tears as Gibbs pushed the tea tray toward them. She waited until he had taken his leave before continuing. "Jonathan started teasing me that Andrew was really back but hiding from me because he didn't want the marriage after all."

"That's ridiculous! And that brother of yours is a cad to even suggest such a thing."

"That's what I told him," Clarissa hiccuped back a sob. "But when he finally saw how truly upset he'd made me, he relented and suggested that Andrew might have taken a private carriage and come directly here." She accepted Emma's offered steaming cup of tea with a trembling hand. "Jonathan said I should just wait and give Andrew time to collect himself before he came to call." She sniffed again. "I know I shouldn't burden you with this, but I just couldn't wait. Are you sure he didn't arrive without your notice?"

"My dear, Andrew would never do anything to cause you such distress. I'm guessing his business took longer than he'd planned and he's penned you a letter stating exactly that. The errant letter will probably arrive days after he does."

"You truly think that that's the case?"

"Of course. I'd even bet that Andrew, being stuck in Atlanta, is just as frustrated as you are."

"I feel like an insecure ninny," Clarissa dabbed at her tears.

Emma picked up the plate of cookies. "Here, have a cookie, drink your tea, then go home and relax. I'm sure he'll be home any day."

Emma didn't let her concern show until Clarissa had departed. It wasn't like her cousin to cause anyone distress, least of all Clarissa. Deciding a quick trip to the telegraph office might solve the mystery, she removed her apron and grabbed her shawl.

∾

WALKING BACK Emma remembered that her new tenant had mentioned dining with Andrew on several occasions. She'd have to speak with Mr. Thompson when next she saw him. But the notion went right out of her mind when Agatha Milksop stood at the balcony railing and yelled "Bandit! Bandit! …you get in here this instant."

Shaking her head, Emma walked quickly up the stairs. What she didn't need was her other guests or the neighbors to think there was an actual bandit on the premises. But as she reached the top a thumping sound came from Aunt Daisy's room, making Emma change directions.

"For goodness sake, what are you doing?" Aunt Daisy was standing in the center of her room, jumping up and down, flapping her hands and making squeaking noises. She looked as if she were trying to fly and she sounded like a mouse in distress. Getting no response, Emma stepped in front of her and reached for her hands. This caused the woman to jump even higher and "baaaa ah ah." It seemed she could not decide whether to emulate a bird, a mouse, or a lamb.

Tears came to Emma's eyes as she tried to keep from laughing out loud. "Calm down, Auntie. It was Admiral Worthington again, wasn't it?"

Admiral Theodore Worthington was Wakefield House's resident ghost. Tellingly, he seldom bothered anyone other than Daisy.

Daisy stopped her bouncing. "It certainly was not! This one touched me. Touched me!"

Emma led her husband's great aunt through the open porch and into her private parlor. "Here, sit down. Tell me all about it. I'll get us something to drink."

"I don't want tea," Daisy huffed.

"It's not tea I'm getting." Emma reached into a low cupboard and withdrew two glasses and the bottle of fine whiskey she kept solely for these occasions. The bottle was half empty.

Daisy accepted the glass and drained it in one gulp. "I was in my room minding my own business when I felt a cold hand on my shoulder." A chill ran through her. "I turned, and there he was."

"Admiral Worthington?"

"No, the ghost. Emma dear, you simply must pay attention."

"What did he look like?"

"A ghost. What do you think he looked like?"

Emma took a long draught of her own whiskey. "But you said it wasn't Worthington so you must have seen some difference."

"Worthington looks like Worthington. This one looked like a ghost," Daisy declared. "You're too rational, my dear. You really must get over that. It's not becoming."

Emma had no hope of responding. "Let me go back to your room to see if anything is amiss," she offered.

"We'll go together," Daisy insisted, and the two of them, whiskey enabled, approached Daisy's door. As Emma opened it, a furry creature ran over their feet and both ladies let out a shriek. "Bandit," Emma cried, "what were you doing in there?" Unsurprisingly, the cat did not answer.

Daisy's room looked quite as it should, but Emma took notice of the white shawl which hung on a peg over the bureau and how that shawl was reflected in the mirror across the room. She could well imagine Bandit playing behind the shawl. The reflection might well have resembled a ghost.

"Nothing here now," Emma said.

"I suppose you think it was the cat," Daisy accused. "Well I can certainly tell the difference between a ghost and a cat."

"Of course you can," Emma assured her. She did not add "But what if the cat was wearing a shawl?"

~

EMMA FROWNED as she went over her ledger for the third time. She'd never had a problem with figures but today, no matter how she calculated, the totals would not match the cash she had on hand. Somehow she was missing money. Not a huge amount but enough to make her take notice. She counted the cash again, carefully separating each bill from the last, hoping one might have stuck to another. The total remained the same. Not sure what to think, she made her notations and readied the deposits for the bank.

The door to her office flew open with a bang, making her jump as Aunt Daisy rushed in. "Emma, there's a thief in the house. My jewelry box…" she stammered, "it's missing."

"Show me." Emma felt her anger grow even as she wondered who could be so cold as to steal from someone as sweet as Aunt Daisy.

They entered Daisy's room and the old woman pointed to the empty place of honor on her dresser. "It's gone." Her eyes filled with tears. "My grandmother gave that to me when I turned sixteen."

Emma glanced about the room then took a breath of relief when she spied the ornately carved box half hidden under a throw on Daisy's bed. "Auntie," she stepped further into the room and reached for the box. "It's here."

Aunt Daisy looked confused. "What is it doing on the bed? I always keep it on the dresser."

Emma urged Daisy into a chair and placed the box in her lap. "Perhaps you'd better check inside to see if anything is missing."

"The lock has been tampered with," she said as she opened the box.

"I think I did that," Emma said gently.

"Emma dear if you wanted to borrow something you had

only to ask." Daisy poked through the tangle of jewelry in the box.

"Um, I believe I did that a few weeks ago when you told me you couldn't find the key but you wanted to wear your mother's cameo."

For a moment Daisy looked confused then her eyes brightened. "Oh I remember that. The key was nowhere to be found and you cleverly picked the lock."

"So, is everything there?"

Daisy shook her head. "My bracelet is missing. You know, the gold one that I always wear." She held up her wrist that indeed had no bracelet.

"Is there anything else?" Emma strove to keep her anger from showing.

"And I don't believe my mother's cameo is here." She passed the carved box to Emma. "That's my best piece of jewelry. Here you look."

Emma placed the box back on the dresser. The cameo was indeed missing also. "I don't see it," she said finally. "Auntie," she said as she turned to survey the room. "Let's move the box to someplace less obvious. Perhaps in your wardrobe."

"Why would I want to do that?"

"Just until I can find out who's been helping themselves to your jewelry."

"Oooh," Daisy's smile returned. "Make it more difficult for the thief to find it."

"Exactly." Emma opened the wardrobe door and moving Daisy's shoes aside placed the box on the bottom shelf. "And you want to be sure you keep your door locked." She turned as a loud meow sounded from the open doorway.

"Here Bandit," Daisy called as the cat jumped up to sit in her lap. He turned in a circle then plopped down and began to purr loudly.

"The Milksops have got to keep a better watch on that cat," Emma declared. For a moment she wondered if the cat could have gotten into the jewelry box then dismissed the idea as ridiculous. "Do you want me to get him out of here for you?"

"Oh no," Daisy continued to stroke the purring animal. "He often comes in to keep me company."

"But you're going to remember to keep your door locked?"

"Um hum," Daisy responded, not bothering to look up.

"I'm going to go to the market and then to the bank. Will you be all right here?"

"Go do your errands, dear," Daisy said gently stroking the cat. "Bandit and I will be fine."

Emma stepped out on the balcony and quietly closed the door behind her. First money from her office and now jewelry from Aunt Daisy's room. She stood for a moment trying to decide what to do. Henny was her newest staff member. Had she been too hasty when she hired the young girl? Henny came with no references but Emma had learned that the girl's family had fallen on hard times. Had she let that knowledge override her common sense?

Deciding she needed to keep a better eye on her young maid, Emma tucked her basket over her arm and joined Sadie as the two walked the three blocks to the open market on Charlotte Street. Enjoying the January weather, she turned her face toward the refreshing sea breeze that gently stirred the palm trees. They reached the market and made their way down the aisle where bushels of produce were arranged to tempt even the most cautious buyer.

Emma let Sadie do the selecting. The woman had an eye for picking only the ripest pieces. Emma's mouth watered as she passed a newly arrived shipment of Damson plums. Sadie made the best plum preserves she'd ever tasted. And after seeing the quantity that Sadie had selected, Emma knew a plum tart would soon be on their dinner menu. Looking around Emma wondered if Willie would appear to assist Sadie with her purchases. She was about to ask when a commotion the next aisle over claimed her attention. A rude patron was causing quite a disturbance as he haggled with a fishmonger over the quality of his catch.

Emma frowned and stepped to the side for a better look, but Sadie blocked her way. "Who is that awful man?" Emma asked, as his curses filled the air.

"That be Frank Jefferson," Sadie said with disgust. "Willie's father."

"That man is Willie's father?"

Sadie took Emma's arm to turn her away. "When he's not working down at the docks, that man's a drunk and a scoundrel of the worst kind. You don't need to be listening to the likes of him."

Emma shook her head but let Sadie steer her in the opposite direction. "A man like that doesn't deserve a boy like Willie," she said sadly.

"That's the honest truth," Sadie agreed. "Don't forget Mrs. Acosta asked for some Winslow's Soothing Syrup for her little one. Seems he's started teething and that's the cause of all the crying of late."

Emma nodded. "I'll pick that up after I stop at the bank. I haven't seen Willie about today. Will you be able to fetch everything yourself?"

Sadie smiled. "You go on and finish those errands. And you might stop at the Confectionery Shop and try that new milk punch everyone is so excited about."

Emma just shook her head.

"I mean that, Mrs. Wakefield," Sadie chided. "With Wakefield House filling up, you never take a moment for yourself these days."

"I'm fine, Sadie." Emma patted the woman's arm before she turned to go. Wakefield House was indeed filling, she thought with delight. But someone had helped themselves to money from her office and Aunt Daisy's bracelet and cameo.

Emma made her way to the bank and prayed it wouldn't be long before Andrew responded to her telegram.

CHAPTER 3

*E*mma entered the St. Augustine Bank and smiled as two tellers looked out from the grid work over their respective counters. But before she could offer a "good afternoon," Milton Forbes, the bank's owner, quickly rose from his desk and rounded the counter to greet her.

A rotund man, Emma often wondered why, with all his wealth, he never managed to wear clothing that fit properly. His vest gaped with buttons that always appeared in danger of taking flight.

She'd had it on good authority that the man liked to nap after his noon day meal and she purposely tried to time her visits when he wasn't on site. But today she wasn't in luck.

"My dear Mrs. Wakefield," Forbes reached for her hand. "Whatever brings you to my door?"

Wishing she wore gloves, Emma took the clammy hand he extended. "I'm simply making a deposit, Mr. Forbes," she said, trying unsuccessfully to extract her hand from his. "There is no need for you to disturb yourself. I'm sure one of your tellers will be more than able to assist me."

"Nonsense," Forbes gently tugged her toward his desk.

"You must sit for a spell and tell me all about your little business venture. I'm sure I could offer you some well-thought-out advice. And of course for you, my dear, there would be no charge."

Grateful that he finally released her hand, Emma perched on one of the wooden chairs that faced his massive mahogany desk while Forbes seated himself behind. "My business is doing quite well," she began, hating that she felt compelled to explain herself. "We are nearly full and there are still months left in the season. I have every confidence that Wakefield House will continue as a success."

"Hmmmm," Forbes steepled his pudgy fingers as he leaned back in his chair. "It's not wise to become over confident, Mrs. Wakefield, not wise at all. I think you would do well to let me oversee the finances for you."

Emma stiffened. "That's a kind offer, but I'm sure I can manage. Now if you will excuse me, I do need to make this deposit and return. I have guests who will be wanting their supper."

"A woman of your station shouldn't be concerned with getting meals for others," Forbes tsked.

Emma stood. "Thank you for your concern, Mr. Forbes, but it's misplaced. Now, please excuse me. I have other errands to attend to."

"Let me take you for a meal," Forbes rose as Emma nimbly backed away from his desk.

"Thank you," she gave a slight nod, "but I must decline."

"Surely your husband has been dead long enough for you to start socializing again."

Emma froze and turned back to face Forbes who still stood behind his desk. "Thank you for your concern but no thank you for the invitation." Reaching the counter, she thrust her deposit at the clerk who was careful to keep his face averted. When he offered her receipt, she nodded a quick thanks then stuffed it into her reticule.

"I'll stop by to check on your progress in a day or two," Forbes called after her as she stalked out of the bank.

She'd marched nearly a block before her anger abated. Stopping to take a breath she felt her cheeks burn. Why, she asked herself again, was there only one banking establishment in town? Forcing herself to take several deep breaths, she continued her walk at a more reasonable pace.

Milton Forbes had been at her door just days after news had spread of her husband's death. His offer of financial assistance had been a thinly veiled desire to acquire her home. Well not in this lifetime, she thought. I don't care what I have to do, but Wakefield House will be a success. Forcing herself to continue at a more relaxed pace, she made her way to the pharmacy to pick up some Winslow's Soothing Syrup for Mrs. Acosta.

EMMA HURRIED to her bedroom and removed her Sunday bonnet. Donning her apron she made her way quickly to the dining room to check the setup for dinner. The pastor had been long-winded today and she felt more than a little pressed for time. Her mood lightened as she entered the room. Thank heavens for Gibbs, Henny and dear Sadie, she thought. The places were set and the flowers she'd arranged early that morning sat proudly in the center of each table. Walking through the room she took in each detail. The white table coverings were pristine and finely starched, the water goblets sparkled in the sunlight and the aroma of roasted turkey drifted in from the kitchen.

Suddenly a loud commotion shattered her concentration. Minutes before the main meal of the day was not the time to have a disaster, especially not in the kitchen. She rushed across the lawn to the kitchen and found her entire staff clustered around young Willie. Everyone was speaking at once.

"It's broken," Henny stated emphatically.

"If he can move it, it isn't broken," Sadie argued, ignoring the kettle that hissed on the stove.

"What is going on here?" Emma demanded. The room went suddenly silent. She stepped closer to see an ashen faced Willie perched on a stool. "Willie, what happened?"

"I'm sorry, Mrs. Wakefield," the boy clutched his left arm to his chest with his right hand. "I just fell. I came to ask Sadie if she could give me some tea for the pain. I'd gladly chop wood or carry the market baskets as payment."

"Don't be ridiculous." Emma moved closer, noting again how threadbare his trousers were and how the sleeve of his shirt had come apart at the shoulder. "What did you do to your arm?"

Willie's pale cheeks flushed with color. "I just fell," he stammered.

But on closer examination Emma couldn't help but notice the bruise that was growing just above his eye.

"That ain't from no fall," Tobias, the gardener, said quietly. "That bruise be from someone's fist."

Emma turned back to Willie. "Were you in a fight?"

Willie bowed his head, "No ma'am, I just fell is all."

"Well it doesn't matter how it happened but something needs doing to that arm," Aunt Daisy declared. "Henny, get me my needle and thread."

Now Willie looked up in alarm. "I just need some tea or something to make the ache go away," he said desperately. "I don't mean to cause trouble and I'll pay for whatever you can spare me."

"Enough," Emma said, as everyone again started giving

suggestions as to what would help the boy's arm. "Henny, go fetch Doctor Grayson. He should be coming down to dinner any moment. Ask him if he'd join us here. Gibbs, return to the dining room and see to the serving of dinner. Aunt Daisy, please help Sadie and Tobias move the food. We have a house full of guests who are probably already wondering where their noonday meal is."

As everyone scurried to do her bidding, Emma stepped forward and brushed the hair back from Willie's forehead. The boy flinched and shook his hair back into place. "I don't need no doctor," he said quickly, clearly embarrassed by her action.

"Who doesn't need a doctor?" They both turned as Alexander Grayson stepped into the kitchen carrying his medical bag. The doctor had only been in residence a few weeks but his dashing good looks yet quiet demeanor already had the local mothers trying their hand at matchmaking. "What seems to be the problem here?" he asked, setting his bag on the work table.

"I don't need no doctor!" Willie insisted trying to rise from the stool where he sat. But Emma's firm hand on his head kept him in place.

"You've hurt your arm?" Grayson asked, moving closer. He removed his coat and, not sure where to lay it, handed it to Emma.

"It's broken," Aunt Daisy said entering the kitchen to retrieve a tureen of gopher-turtle stew.

"It probably needs to be stitched up," Henny added, picking up a dish of boiled turnips and carrots.

Willie clenched his injured arm more tightly to his chest.

Grayson pulled a stool over to sit in front of the boy who was now trembling. "Why don't you let me take a look at it," he said gently. "I'm sure we can put you to rights again." Carefully he pried Willie's good hand away. "Can you move your fingers?" he asked, never taking his eyes off the boy's arm." Willie complied but winced in pain from the motion.

Gently the doctor eased the arm from the boy's chest making Willie cry out in pain. "Just take a deep breath," he said quietly as his fingers moved deftly up and down the arm. Satisfied, he looked up at Emma who was now almost as white as Willie. "The lad is right. The arm isn't broken," he said firmly. "I believe it's dislocated from his shoulder."

"Dislocated?" Emma stammered.

"It ain't gonna fall off is it?" Willie cried in alarm.

"No, nothing like that," the doctor smiled. "And we can fix it in a jiffy."

"What are you going to do to me? I don't want nobody sewing on me."

Grayson now had one hand on Willie's wrist and his other on the boy's elbow. He glanced down toward the floor and shouted, "Snake!"

Both Emma and Willie turned their heads in fright and the doctor gave Willie's shoulder a sharp snap.

Willie cried out in pain. "Aaarrr!"

"Where's the snake?" Emma, still clutching the doctor's coat, had pulled her skirts tightly about her, glancing at the floor for the culprit.

Grayson only grinned as he stood. "Sorry," he said, not looking at all apologetic. "I guess I was mistaken. Willie," he turned to the boy who was now moving his arm in amazement, "how does it feel now?"

The boy looked up at him with eyes as big as saucers. "Geez, what did you do? The pain's nearly gone." Gingerly he extended his arm. "And it works again."

"Your arm came undone from your shoulder. I just popped it back into place."

Willie tentatively moved his arm from side to side and a huge grin split his face. "It works almost good as new," he said. Then his grin faded. "I ain't got enough coins on me to pay you," he said slowly. "But I…"

Grayson held up a hand to stop the boy's words. "No payment necessary, lad. Now, you need to have a care with it for the next few days so it doesn't pop out again."

"Does he need a sling?" Emma asked, stepping closer. "Something to keep his arm from coming undone again?"

"Nothing that drastic," Grayson said with a smile. "Just have a care lad and you should be fine. But to be on the safe side I'd not go lifting anything too heavy for the next few days."

Willie's grin was back. "Thanks Doc." He nodded to Emma, "Mrs. Wakefield. I'll be off then."

"Wait," Emma glanced around and spotting a wooden bowl with apples and oranges, plucked two of each and put them in one of Sadie's small grocery sacks. "Here, take this with you. You need to keep your strength up so the good doctor's work doesn't come undone."

Blushing, Willie accepted the sack and with a nod was off.

Emma turned back to the doctor. "Thank you for helping him. If there truly is a fee, I'll be glad to pay it for him."

Alex shook his head as he reached for his coat. "That's not necessary but I am concerned. That shoulder wasn't the result of a fall."

Emma sighed. "I was afraid of that." She started to say more but Gibbs stepped into the kitchen doorway.

"Dinner is served, Madam."

Reluctantly the doctor picked up his bag. "Then I'd best get to my seat before Captain Delgado claims more than his share of Sadie's gopher-turtle stew. It's a favorite of mine." He smiled wryly, "and of his." With a nod he left the kitchen.

For a moment Emma stood motionless wondering what had just happened to her. While holding the doctor's coat she'd had the craziest desire to press her face against the soft

35

fabric and inhale his clean male scent. Whatever had she been thinking? But her thoughts scattered when Aunt Daisy stepped back into the kitchen with her sewing kit.

"Where did the boy go? I told him that needed stitching."

Emma choked back a laugh. "Doctor Grayson fixed the arm but it didn't need stitching."

Now Daisy blinked in surprise. "Good heavens, girl, I wasn't talking about his arm. It's the shirt that needed mending. Didn't you see how the sleeve was rent from the shoulder?"

Emma nodded. "You have a good heart, Aunt Daisy. But Willie's gone and right now you need to join the others in the dining room and enjoy your noonday meal."

Daisy picked up her sewing basket and rolled her eyes. "Isn't right to let the lad go running around with a torn shirt. And why is it called the noonday meal when we hardly ever sit down at noon?" Then, still muttering to herself, Daisy left the kitchen.

LATER WHEN THE meal had been consumed and tables cleared, Emma retreated to her private parlor. Her usual habit was to invite her guests to join her for an afternoon of cards or conversation but today she felt the need to be alone. Aunt Daisy had been fretting about an impending disaster ever since she'd found a black feather on her way to church service that morning. Emma had tried to convince her that the disaster had been Willie's dislocated shoulder, but Daisy wasn't to be put off.

"You mark my words, Emma," the old woman declared in a voice of doom. "Something terrible is going to happen. You wait and see. When a crow loses a feather, it's an omen."

Emma settled in her favorite overstuffed chair and tried to suppress a shiver. Usually she could ignore Daisy's gloomy prophecies but today she couldn't shake her own feeling of unrest. Deciding that the best solution was to take her mind off Daisy, poor Willie's arm and everything else, she reached for her secret vice: a stack of penny dreadful magazines she kept hidden under a large atlas that rested on the lower shelf of her side table. Reaching down, she pulled out an issue, settled back in her chair and started her escape.

She was deep in the forest of Transylvania when a firm knock sounded on her door. Recognizing the summons to be Gibbs, she hastily replaced the magazine and slid the atlas back into place before calling for him to enter.

"Madam," Gibbs said, stepping into the room, "a telegram just arrived." He handed Emma the folded note but as he turned to leave, her gasp stopped him. "Madam?"

Emma looked up from the telegram as the blood drained from her face. "Andrew checked out of his hotel on schedule - days ago."

Gibbs took a step closer. "Should you tell Miss Clarissa?"

Emma stood and began to pace. "Not until I know what is going on. I know his mother has been feeling poorly, but if I inquire and he didn't travel there, I'll only make his parents worry unnecessarily. If I knew how to reach Howard, Andrew's older brother, I'd contact him. but I haven't a clue where he is at the moment." She reread the telegram and continued to pace. "I have to do something…."

"Should you report him missing to his office?"

Emma shook her head. "I wouldn't want to do that and then find Andrew is perfectly okay and I embarrassed him for no reason."

"But if he is in some type of trouble…."

"Jonathan!" she said suddenly.

"Miss Clarissa's brother?"

"Exactly. He already knows Clarissa is upset with Andrew's delay so I'm positive he'd be willing to help. I'll go over to the Campbell's and see if I can speak with Jonathan privately."

"May I make a suggestion, madam?" Emma stopped on her way to the door. "If you arrive at the Campbell's, Miss Clarissa is sure to know. Why don't you let me send a message asking Mr. Jonathan to attend you here?"

"You're right of course," Emma slipped the telegram into her pocket. "Until we know what is truly going on, I don't want to cause Clarissa any more distress."

"Then if you'll pen a message, I'll see that it's delivered immediately."

JONATHAN CAMPBELL ARRIVED at Wakefield House within the hour. Whereas Clarissa was petite and blond, Jonathan was tall and shared the dark hair color of their father.

"What's this all about?" he asked when Gibbs led him to Emma's parlor on the second floor.

Emma pulled the telegram from her pocket and handed it to him. She watched as he read the note several times before handing it back.

"Do you think he's in some type of trouble?"

"I don't know. Should I contact his office?"

Jonathan shook his head. "No, I wouldn't do that. He'd be embarrassed if he was just taking a few days of rest before returning home to my sister and all her wedding plans. She can drive a body crazy with the details. I know that first hand."

"But you also know he'd never worry Clarissa like this, and now I'm worried too."

Jonathan gazed about the room as if looking for answers. "Do you think he went up to New York to visit his parents before the upcoming nuptials?"

"I thought of that, but you know how punctual Andrew is.

If he were going to change his plans he would have sent your sister a telegram. It's the fact that we haven't heard from him that has me so concerned."

"You're right. As much as I like to tease her, Andrew would never do anything to upset her. Do you have any ideas?"

Emma took a deep breath. "I was hoping I could persuade you to travel to Atlanta to see if you could find out something. All we know is that he checked out of his hotel as planned. I know it's a lot to ask but…"

"If he left Atlanta, at some point he'd come down the St John's River past Jacksonville, then get off at Tocoi Landing. I can travel back that way and see what information I can find."

"Could you leave tomorrow?"

"No, I'll leave this afternoon. If Langley is in trouble, there's no sense in waiting another day. If he's not, I'll just knock some sense into him for causing you and my sister this worry, then we'll have a drink or two."

Emma reached for Jonathan's hand. "You'll be careful?"

He pulled her close for a quick hug. "Don't worry about me. I'll be fine."

EMMA AWOKE with a start as lightning flashed, illuminating every corner of her bedroom. Her heart pounding, she sat up in bed and counted slowly to herself until she heard the rumble of thunder off in the distance. Just a storm, she muttered, trying to settle herself again under the covers. But when lightning flashed again, she knew she'd never find sleep. Resigning herself to the inevitable, she rose and donned her wrapper. Not bothering with slippers, she quietly made her way to the door of her room.

Stepping out onto the balcony she took a deep breath. The air carried the scent of the coming rain as thunder sounded closer this time. The wind picked up and tree tops began to sway in the breeze. Truth be told, she had never minded storms. As a youth, she had enjoyed many an afternoon sitting on her family's front porch watching the rain. But those days were long gone and her responsibilities now left little time for an idle afternoon. She moved to the railing and leaned out. The storm was definitely getting closer and her unbound hair whipped around in a dance all its own as the wind intensified.

A movement in the shadow of the stairwell brought a cry to her lips, but she swallowed it back as Dr. Grayson appeared. Emma clutched her hand against her chest to calm her heart which felt like it might explode from the fright.

"I'm sorry," the doctor said as lightning flashed again, illuminating his form. "I didn't mean to frighten you. I wasn't expecting to see anyone up this late, let alone outside."

"It's going to rain," Emma stammered, trying to find her wits and her voice at the same time.

"Yes, I expect it is." He smiled. "Is there something wrong?"

"Why would you think there was something wrong?"

"Well," he moved closer. "It's after midnight, and as you said it's going to rain." The sky opened as he spoke, forcing them to move back from the balcony rail.

Lightning flashed brightly and Emma was suddenly aware of how very tired the doctor looked.

"Are you just getting home?"

Dr. Grayson nodded. "I was called to help with the delivery of the Brennen's baby. The midwife realized there were complications and sent Mr. Brennen to fetch me."

"And?" Lightning flashed again and seeing the expression on his face, Emma was sorry she had asked.

Alex wearily shook his head. "The cord was wrapped too tightly around the child's neck. We weren't able to save him."

In sympathy, Emma reached out and laid her hand on the doctor's arm. "I'm so sorry. Would you like me to make you a cup of coffee or mug of tea?"

Alex looked down where her hand rested then up at her. But this time when the lightning flashed it was instantly chased with a clap of thunder so loud that both Emma and Dr. Grayson jumped with a start.

The cry of a baby drifted on the air and Emma turned to see a light begin to glow in the Acosta's room at the end of the balcony.

"I guess we're not the only ones still up," Alex said, never taking his eyes from Emma's face.

The wind changed direction and rain now danced on the edge of the balcony. Emma shivered and clutched her wrapper more tightly around her. "You should go in," Alex said quietly. "We're both going to get wet if we stay out much longer and you don't even have your slippers on."

Emma felt her cheeks grow hot as she realized she was standing in front of the doctor with bare feet, wearing only her night dress and wrapper. The baby's angry wails subsided and they both turned as the light at the end of the balcony once more went out. "You're right," she said, hoping he didn't notice how breathless she sounded. "Morning will soon be upon us. I'll bid you good night." Turning, she quickly made her way back into the safety of her own room.

Now she realized her feet were freezing as she shed her wrapper. Shivering violently, she climbed under the covers to find warmth and to still her racing heart.

CHAPTER 4

*I*t was still dark when Emma entered the dining room and turned the oil lamps up brighter for breakfast. Henny had already set the table and the scent of coffee and bacon was heavy in the air. As usual, Captain Delgado was the first to take his place at the table.

"Good morning, Mrs. Wakefield."

Emma smiled in greeting at one of her favorite guests, then poured his coffee. "I trust the storm didn't bother you overmuch last night."

The Captain picked up the mug with a grateful sigh. "I've slept through cannon fire," he replied. "A minor storm doesn't wake me."

Bertram Hartnell's cologne entered the room before him. He was a round little man who combed his thin strands of hair from one side to the other in a desperate attempt to hide his balding head. "Then you're fortunate," he said, joining the Captain at the table. "Damn thing kept me awake half the night. I need to be off this morning but I can't keep my eyes open. How can I sell my wares when I'm too sleepy to read my own labels?"

"Then this should help," Emma said handing him a mug filled with coffee just the way he preferred, heavy with cream and sugar.

"Did the storm cause much damage?" the Captain asked.

"A lot of branches down, but the boys will have them cleared as soon as it's light," Emma replied.

Gibbs entered with a platter of boiled ham with eggs and potatoes. Sadie followed with a bowl of grits and a platter of sausages. "The fish will be served directly, Mrs. Wakefield," Sadie said, placing the platters on the sideboard.

"Are we just two this morning?" Hartnell rose from the table to load his plate.

"I'm afraid so…" Emma started but was interrupted when the church bell rang out.

"This is rather early for a service, isn't it?" Hartnell asked, resuming his place at the table, his plate now fully loaded. "I mean it's barely six."

The Captain set down his mug and sighed. "The bell rings when a resident has passed over."

"Dear Lord," Hartnell gasped, crossing himself. "I meant no disrespect."

"You didn't know," Emma said quietly. "The doctor told me that the Brennens lost a child last night."

"They're the death tolls," the Captain added. "The bell will ring at six in the morning, at noon, and again at six in the evening."

"Then I shan't be sorry to be away today. Would it be possible to get a basket to take with me, Mrs. Wakefield, since I'll be absent for the noonday meal?"

"I'll see to it, Mr. Hartnell. I'm sure Sadie will be able to pack you a suitable repast."

Emma made her way to the kitchen as Henny stepped out laden with a breakfast tray complete with a coffee urn, a mug, and biscuits with ham. "What are you doing?" Emma asked moving in front of the girl.

"It's for Mr. Thompson, ma'am," Henny said, shifting the heavy tray. "He asked if I might bring something to break the fast to his room each morning."

"I see…"

"It's all right, isn't it?" she asked nervously.

"Certainly, Henny" Emma reassured. "I'm just surprised Mr. Thompson didn't tell me of his request."

"He mentioned that. He said you was busy with Miss Campbell and he didn't want to bother you. And would I mind fetching for him. I don't mind at all, him being so handsome and everything."

Emma watched the young girl's cheeks grow pink. "Then by all means take the tray. But don't dawdle. Sadie needs you in the kitchen."

"Yes, ma'am," Henny nodded then started quickly down the path to the house.

Emma continued to the kitchen to find Gibbs, Sadie, and Tobias enjoying their own breakfast.

"You be wanting your tea now?" Sadie asked, rising from the table.

"No, finish your breakfast, Sadie. I can certainly pour a cup of tea myself. Has Aunt Daisy been down yet?"

Sadie sat and shook her head. "Lately she's been waiting till the Acostas come down so she can hold their baby."

"Oh dear," Emma muttered.

"No cause for alarm." Sadie placed a small dish of eggs in front of Emma. "She holds the baby so Mrs. Acosta can eat in peace. Sure is a shame about their house fire."

"They were lucky to get out alive," Gibbs added. "But the mister showed me the plans for their new home and it's going to be quite grand."

Emma sipped her tea. "I'm glad they'll be staying with us

until their construction is complete." She turned to Tobias as he rose from the table. "Will you see to the wood pile today? It's lower than I'm comfortable with."

Tobias nodded. "Yes, ma'am. I'll be seeing to the garden this morning after I clear away the storm branches. I'll get to the wood pile this afternoon for certain."

"And while you're out there see that you stay out of my garden," Sadie warned. "I'll see to it myself in a bit." She turned back to Emma. "I'm hoping the storm last night didn't do too much harm."

Later that day, Emma carried a strawberry pie to the sideboard and smiled with satisfaction. As usual, Sadie had outdone herself and the guests were bound to be pleased with the noon offering. Venison stew, fried pork chops, and a roasted turkey filled the sideboard along with a variety of mouth-watering vegetable dishes.

Mr. and Mrs. Acosta chatted with Aunt Daisy as she held their new baby, while Dr. Grayson spoke with Captain Delgado. Mr. Thompson was the last to arrive and took his seat just as the church bells rang out.

"I say," he looked at Emma. "Didn't those bells ring rather early this morning?"

"Those are death knells," Captain Delgado explained.

"The Brennens lost a child last night," Dr. Grayson added.

"Oh, how horrible," Mrs. Acosta gasped. "Was there an accident?"

"It was a stillbirth," the doctor said quietly.

"I'm so sorry to hear that. But this isn't proper conversation for…" Her words were interrupted when the bells rang a second time.

Startled, Emma jerked and sent the coffee pot crashing to the floor. "Oh no…"

Dr. Grayson was out of his seat and at her side in a flash. "Are you burned?" he asked. Taking the cloth from her hand he retrieved the pot from where it lay on the floor.

"Did something fall?" Gibbs entered the dining room with another platter of food.

"I'm too clumsy," Emma stammered. "And no, I'm not burned. I just wasn't expecting the second church bell."

"Bad news all round," Gibbs said, taking the coffee pot from the doctor. "I'll have this filled directly." He looked at Emma. "And I'll send Henny in to clean the spill."

"That means another soul has crossed over," Aunt Daisy said, rocking the baby a little faster. "I hope it's not someone we know."

But as Emma made her way back to the kitchen, she couldn't shake the sense of dread that had settled on her shoulders.

EMMA WAS CHECKING the flowers she'd placed in the parlor when Gibbs entered. One look at his face confirmed her worst fears.

"A runner just came from the Campbell's," he said quietly.

"Oh no, Andrew?"

Gibbs nodded and Emma couldn't stop the tears that instantly filled her eyes. She pressed a hand to her heart and swayed.

Rushing forward, Gibbs gently took her arm and led her to the closest chair. "I'm so sorry...should I fetch Miss Daisy for you?"

"I say," Samuel Thompson stepped into the parlor. "Is everything all right? I thought I heard..." Seeing Emma he quickly came to her side. "Mrs. Wakefield, my dear, what is wrong?"

Embarrassed to be so distressed in front of one of her guests, Emma struggled to stem her tears. "Forgive me, Mr.

Thompson," she dabbed at her eyes with her hanky. "We just received some dreadful news."

"Here," Gibbs passed her a tumbler with a finger of whiskey, "drink this."

Emma took the glass but didn't drink.

"Nothing to do with those church bells I pray," Thompson continued.

"I'm afraid so." Emma sniffed and sat up straighter. "Mr. Campbell just sent word that Mr. Langley…" Emma found that she couldn't continue.

"Mr. Langley's dead? My God! No wonder you're upset."

"Oh no! Clarissa," Emma said, standing so quickly she almost spilled the drink. "I've got to go to her."

"Then let me get a carriage and accompany you," Thompson offered. "After all, Langley and I were friends. It's the least I can do." He turned to Gibbs. "Can you hire a carriage for me?"

Gibbs looked at Emma who nodded. "I'll see to it directly."

Within the hour Emma and Thompson were in a carriage making their way to the Campbell residence.

"What business are the Campbells in?" Thompson asked, breaking the silence.

"Excuse me?"

"I mean is it old family money?"

"I'm sure I don't know," Emma stated flatly, stunned that he would begin such an offensive line of conversation.

"I only ask because as I walked the city trying to learn my way around, I couldn't help but notice that the Campbell home was one of the grandest."

"The Campbells have lived here for more than three generations," Emma replied stiffly, then pointedly turned her head away.

"I meant no disrespect," Thompson continued. "I only

asked so I would know how best to offer my condolences to the family." Emma turned back to look at him. "What I meant was that if they are running a business, then I could offer to lend my services during this difficult time so the family wouldn't be bothered with inconsequential details while they are grieving. I certainly didn't mean to imply anything improper, Mrs. Wakefield."

Embarrassed that she'd thought the worst, Emma sighed. "I'm sure the family would be appreciative of any offer, Mr. Thompson. That's very considerate of you."

Relieved when the carriage reached the Campbell home, Emma allowed Thompson to help her down. The home was indeed the grandest in St. Augustine, with exposed coquina walls protected by deep, wrap-around verandas and second floor balconies. But she stopped abruptly when she realized there wasn't a black wreath on the door. For the briefest moment she allowed herself to hope that the information had been wrong, that Andrew wasn't dead and it had all been a ghastly mistake. Then reality took hold. Since Clarissa and Andrew hadn't formally announced their engagement, he wouldn't be considered family. There would be no black wreath.

The front door opened as they walked up the steps and Emma could tell by the expression on Watson's, face, that there hadn't been a mistake after all.

"Mrs. Wakefield," the butler said, bidding them to enter "may I announce you and your companion?"

"I came as soon as I heard," Emma said. "Is Miss Clarissa receiving?"

"No, madam, but Mr. Campbell and Mr. Jonathan are in the family parlor. Mr. Jonathan saw your carriage arrive and alerted me. May I take you back?" He looked questioningly at Thompson then back to Emma.

"This is Mr. Thompson, Watson," Emma said. "He was a friend of Mr. Langley's."

Watson nodded. "This way then." He led them to the family parlor toward the back of the house. French doors had been opened to allow the afternoon breeze to stir the air.

Randolph Campbell stood ramrod straight before a massive fireplace. He was an imposing man, well over six feet in height, with a full head of black hair now liberally streaked with gray. He had the same striking blue eyes as his daughter, but today they flashed not with grief but anger.

"Mrs. Wakefield and her companion, Mr. Thompson," Watson announced as they entered the parlor.

Campbell stepped forward. "Mrs. Wakefield, how kind of you to come."

"I was so sorry to hear such horrid news, Mr. Campbell. But let me introduce you to Mr. Thompson. He's residing at Wakefield House and knew Mr. Langley."

"I see," Campbell said, extending his hand. "Please come in. Might I offer you a drink?"

"Thank you," Thompson said, gazing around the room. Rich burgundy carpet covered the floor and portraits of the Campbell ancestors filled the walls.

"Nothing for me, thank you," Emma said quickly. "Clarissa...?"

Campbell wearily shook his head. "You can imagine how upset she is."

"She's probably never going to come out of her room again," came a voice from across the room.

Emma turned to see Jonathan standing near the window, a glass in one hand and a bottle in the other. "Jonathan," she crossed the room to join him. "Are you all right?"

He raised his half empty glass in a mock salute. "I'll be better as soon as I finish the bottle. Sure I can't pour you something?"

Emma gently rested her hand on his arm. "Can you tell me what happened? Did Andrew take ill?"

"That would have been easier to understand," he said, taking a gulp of his drink. "No, the son-of-a-bitch went and got himself murdered."

"What?" Emma gasped. Turning slightly, she saw Thompson deep in conversation with Clarissa's father. "What can you tell me? Did it have to do with that counterfeit ring he was dealing with?"

"It doesn't seem so. He was on the road outside of Tocoi on his way back here when he was attacked," Jonathan began haltingly. "He was stabbed and dumped on the side of the road. A coachman spotted his body and had the good grace to take it back to the depot. The police suspect a robbery as none of his possessions were found. But when no one claimed the body, they had no choice but to bury him."

Emma pressed a clenched hand against her pounding heart. "Dear Lord, and you're sure it was Andrew they buried?"

Jonathan shrugged and took another drink. "The postmaster recognized the body as someone who had inquired about the coach the day Andrew would have been there. And the sheriff agreed that although the insects had enjoyed quite a feast, the photo I showed was indeed their dead victim. He didn't know that Langley was an agent with the Secret Service since he didn't have any identification and hadn't been working in Tocoi, but he believed me enough to send a telegram to their office to report the murder."

"Why don't you come and sit down," Emma said, leading him to a chair by the window. "I had no idea when I asked for your assistance...."

"Not your fault," Jonathan said wearily. "I truly thought the man was just hiding out for a few days before the engagement was to be announced."

"Oh, … Andrew's parents," Emma struggled to keep her own tears at bay. "This is going to devastate his mother."

"My father sent a telegram to them right after I sent the note to you. But at their age, he doesn't believe they'll be able to make the trip this far south. Although now some of the details of this fiasco are becoming a bit fuzzy." He toasted with his glass again. "I guess we should be grateful that the alligators hadn't found his body or else we'd have never known. When the sheriff started to explain about the insects…."

"Stop," Emma said sharply. "There is no need to remember or repeat any of the grisly details."

"You're right," he said, resting his head on the back of the chair and closing his eyes. "I just wish I didn't have such a vivid imagination."

"Please tell me you didn't share that part of the story with your sister."

Jonathan heaved a sigh. "No, I can't get the images out of my own mind, so I certainly don't want them in hers."

"Daddy?"

Everyone turned to find Clarissa, dressed completely in black, standing in the doorway. Her usual bouncing curls had been pulled back into a severe bun at the nape of her neck but it only served to emphasize the delicate features of her pale face and haunted eyes.

To Emma's surprise, Thompson was the first to reach her side and take her hands in his.

"My dear Miss Campbell, how absolutely horrible this is for you. Allow me to introduce myself, Samuel Thompson. I'm staying at the Wakefield House on the recommendation of my dear friend Mr. Langley. When I heard the terrible news I simply had to join Mrs. Wakefield to express my condolences."

Clarissa produced a wan smile. "How good of you to

come, Mr. Thompson. And Emma, I was sitting outside on the balcony and I thought I heard your voice."

Emma went to her friend then realized that Thompson still held Clarissa's hands in his. "Why don't you come in and sit down," she said gently.

Clarissa allowed Thompson to guide her to the sofa. "They've told you about Andrew," she said quietly as tears traced a silent path down her cheeks.

"Yes, I'm so very sorry," Emma took the seat next to her.

"Did they tell you they'd already buried him?"

Emma could only nod as her throat had become choked with emotion.

"I couldn't even get a lock of his hair to keep..." Clarissa's voice faded to a whisper.

For the next two hours Emma sat next to her friend as neighbors began to call. More than once she thought Clarissa would take her leave and escape to her rooms. But each time she made to retreat, Thompson enticed her back with one more story or anecdote about his experiences with Andrew. And more than once his humorous tales had drawn a smile from the grieving girl. Knowing she could delay no longer, Emma made ready to leave.

"Please don't go," Clarissa begged, holding fast to Emma's hand.

"Darling, I must," Emma said gently, getting to her feet. "I have to see to the supper arrangements for my guests."

"I could stay, if you wish," Thompson offered gallantly. "If I wouldn't be intruding, that is."

"Could you?" Clarissa forced a smile. "You've been such a comfort to me, Mr. Thompson. I'd love for you to share more of your times with Andrew."

"Then it's settled. Mrs. Wakefield will take the carriage back and I can find my own way later."

"Should we expect you for supper tonight then?" Emma asked turning to Thompson.

"Oh no," Clarissa said quickly. "Mr. Thompson, you must stay and dine with us."

Thompson bowed in acceptance. "I shall be honored to join you," he said, neatly slipping onto Emma's spot on the sofa.

Grateful to make her escape, Emma relaxed for the first time in hours as the carriage carried her back to Wakefield House. Who could have known that Mr. Thompson would be such a comfort to her friend? And how was Clarissa going to cope with the loss of her fiancé? The headache that had been threatening all afternoon finally took hold, giving Emma no choice but to let her tears flow. Some were for poor cousin Andrew, some were for Clarissa, but if she were honest, most were for the memories of her own beloved James.

CHAPTER 5

*H*enny checked that the balcony was empty before she unlocked the door to Miss Daisy's room, slipped inside and then quietly closed the door behind her. She knew that Mrs. Wakefield wanted the door to the room open while she was inside cleaning but cleaning was not her goal. She took a moment to survey the room. The jewelry box was missing from its place on the dresser. Not a problem, she thought, as she pulled open the wardrobe door. She'd find it soon enough. But why had the old woman moved it? Had she discovered the missing jewelry already? She'd been counting on the woman's obvious forgetfulness, and she'd never even seen her wear the cameo.

She located the jewelry box on the floor of the wardrobe, half hidden by a shawl that had slipped from its hook. Henny took the shawl and draped it about her shoulders then stood before the looking glass. No, it was too old fashioned. She hung the shawl back on its hook and started opening drawers in the wardrobe. On her third pull she discovered a treasure. Scarves, every color of the rainbow, were jumbled in a heap and filled the small drawer to overflowing. Carefully she pulled out a red one and once again draped it about her shoulders. The fabric was so soft she wondered if it was silk. True, she'd never touched silk before, but surely this was what it must feel like. But when she looked in the mirror the bright color of the scarf only accented how drab the rest of her garments were. Dejected, she pulled it off and shoved it back in the drawer. Then near the bottom of the tangle she spied it: a soft blue-gray scarf the color of morning mist. She tugged it free and rushed back to the mirror.

It took several attempts before she could wind it about her shoulders in a manner that was pleasing. Turning, she studied herself from each direction. Yes, this would do nicely. It complimented her outfit and even matched her eyes if one wasn't too critical.

Picking up Miss Daisy's brush, she removed her cap and straightened her hair, taking a few pins from the dresser tray to hold the stray locks in place. Once again she preened before the mirror. Yes, she thought, this might do the trick. With the scarf and with her hair unbound, Mr. Thompson was sure to look at her the way the doctor gazed at Mrs. Wakefield when he thought she wasn't looking. But I won't be so blind, Henny thought, smiling at her reflection in the mirror. She practiced coquettish smiles and winks looking over her shoulder, then decided she had probably tarried as long as she dared. Moving back to the wardrobe she closed the scarf drawer and then the wardrobe itself. Taking one last look in the mirror, she carefully replaced her cap and pulled the scarf from her shoulders. The fabric was so soft she had no trouble wrapping it into a ball and stuffing it into her apron pocket. Then she eased the door open to check outside. The balcony was empty and she hastily stepped from the room. But before she could turn to re-lock the door, Mrs. Acosta opened her door and stepped out.

"Ah, Henny, is Miss Daisy in her room?"

Henny felt that her heart might leap from her chest. "No ma'am," she stammered.

"Oh," Mrs. Acosta looked at the closed door with confusion. "She's not there?"

"Ah, no ma'am. I was just tidying up in there."

"I see. Then do you know where I might find Mrs. Wakefield?"

Henny tried to appear natural as she edged her way down the balcony. "No ma'am, I'm not sure where she is. Last I saw her, she was in the kitchen but that was a while ago." She watched Mrs. Acosta look back at the closed door to Miss Daisy's room with an expression of confusion on her face. Was she going to say something to Mrs. Wakefield?

"Then if you see Mrs. Wakefield would you tell her I'd like to speak with her?"

"Yes ma'am I'll be sure to tell her." Henny turned and hurried for the stairs. In a pig's eye I'll tell her, she thought. At the base of the stairs, she paused to catch her breath. It didn't matter, she told herself. If Miss Daisy came back and found her room unlocked, she'd just think she'd forgotten to lock it. Besides, once she got Mr. Thompson to truly look at her and realize she was available, she wouldn't need this job anymore anyway. She patted the pocket of her apron that held the scarf and felt her confidence return. Now all she had to do was locate Mr. Thompson when Mrs. Wakefield wasn't around.

~

WILLIE NERVOUSLY MADE his way to the yard behind the woodshed at Wakefield House where his partner in crime, Tobias, awaited him. He didn't have any idea how old the caretaker was, but Willie thought of him as ancient. He did know that Tobias and his wife Sadie had been at Wakefield

House long before it was a boarding house. He looked up into the man's face, dark as a raisin and just as wrinkled.

"Sorry I'm late. I got held up. Old Mrs. Baker can't see too well and asked me to give her an extra hand."

"Ah, I see. No worries, but I got ta get back to the missus. She's been having trouble with the handle of a pot that's comin' loose. I don't wants her to be getting burned cause I didn't get it fixed, so let's get to it."

Just as he handed his tools to Willie, they heard footsteps coming toward them. "Tobias!" Sadie shouted. "What's taking you so long?"

Willie dove behind the wood pile before Sadie rounded the corner of the shed. He crouched there uncomfortably, not daring to move lest the crack of a twig give him away.

For his part, Tobias dared not glance in the direction that Willie had taken. Instead, he took his wife's arm and began to lead her back to the kitchen. "I was just comin'," he told her.

Willie waited until the footsteps faded before rising. With Tobias trapped back in the kitchen, there was no sense in sticking around. He couldn't do any of this alone anyway. He'd just have to get here earlier on the morrow and hope that would work.

~

"MRS. WAKEFIELD, MIGHT I HAVE A WORD?"

Emma paused on the balcony as Sofia Acosta stepped from the room she shared with her husband and son. She was one of the most beautiful women Emma had ever seen. Her golden olive skin always carried a glow, while her deep brown eyes hinted at secrets.

"Certainly, what can I do for you?"

Sofia Acosta smiled. "Oh, I need nothing, but I was

hoping to speak with you. I heard the dreadful news about Mr. Langley, but I didn't realize he was your relative."

"We were cousins," Emma said quietly. "Our mothers were sisters."

Mrs. Acosta reached out and touched Emma gently on the arm. "Then please let me express my condolences for your loss. Mr. Langley was always such a pleasant man. I know he will be missed."

Emma struggled to keep her voice even. All day she had managed to push Andrew's horrible demise from her mind. Now the finality of it was too hard to ignore. "Thank you, Mrs. Acosta. You're right, he will be missed. He was a dear friend as well as a relative." Emma started to turn.

"Oh, one more moment if you will," Mrs. Acosta said quickly. "It's about Miss Daisy."

Before Emma could respond, the woman pulled a gold bracelet from her pocket. "I believe this belongs to her."

"Where…"

"Then it is Miss Daisy's?" she questioned, offering the bracelet to Emma. "I thought it must be. You see I found it tangled in the baby's blanket."

"Oh…"

Mrs. Acosta's smile grew. "You are so fortunate to have one as dear as Miss Daisy. She's been such a help to me with the baby. Sometimes I don't know how I managed without her."

Now Emma smiled. "She is a dear. And I know she adores your little one."

"I believe her bracelet must have come off when she was rocking Ramon," she continued. "But then, as you know, we've had some visitors so I wasn't sure who the bracelet belonged to."

"Daisy is in her room," Emma said, stepping aside. "Would

you like to return it to her? I know she'll be thrilled to get it back."

"I'd…" but before she could say more, the cry of a hungry baby filled the air.

"Don't worry," Emma said, "I'll see that she gets it."

"Thank you." Mrs. Acosta quickly turned to go. "I'm coming," she called softly. "I'm coming, little one."

Emma tucked the bracelet into her pocket. She'd see that it was returned. But where could the cameo be? And she still had no idea who had helped themselves to the money in her office.

Supper over, Emma was passing through the lobby when something hanging from the back of a chair caught her eye. Investigating, she first moved the ottoman, then eased the chair away from the wall. "Damn, damn, damn!" she swore, pounding her hand on the chair with each whispered curse. The entire back of the chair was shredded. The beautiful fabric, imported from England years before, was ruined. Her anger brought tears to her eyes and her jaw began to ache from clenching it.

She took a deep breath. One part of her warned against acting out of anger, another urged her to find and strangle the cat. She chose a third alternative. Without waiting for her anger to subside, she marched up the outdoor stairs, making a deliberate racket as she did so, then pounded on the Milksop's door. Wallace Milksop answered.

"Mrs. Wakefield? Yes?"

"I would like to speak with you and your wife. Now, please."

He pulled the door further open and motioned her to come in. "Agatha dear, Mrs. Wakefield would like to speak with us."

Agatha was sitting across the room in a rocking chair stroking Bandit who was asleep on her lap. "I heard, Wallace. The entire city heard, I am sure."

For a second Emma felt a twinge of guilt for having shouted like a fishwife and wondered if her grief over losing Andrew was making her overreact. "Your cat's scratching has ruined a fine piece of furniture downstairs. That behavior simply cannot be tolerated. You will either have to give him up or give up your lodging here."

Emma stiffened, waiting for the woman to defend the cat or claim it could not be Bandit's doing. But to her complete surprise, Agatha Milksop burst into tears. Pulling a handkerchief from her sleeve she sobbed into the fabric.

Wallace moved to his wife's side and patted her shoulder. "Now Aggie, we don't have to give Bandit up. Surely we can find another place for the winter. It won't be as nice as this, but we will manage. You don't have to give up Bandit."

All the commotion woke Bandit, who sprang from his mistress's lap and bolted for the still-open door as Agatha sobbed.

Wallace grimaced as he struggled unsuccessfully to console his wife. "I am so very sorry about the chair, Mrs. Wakefield." He pulled several large bills from his pocket. "I do hope this will cover the damage."

Emma took the bills without hesitation but she did not speak.

"I wonder if we might give Bandit a second chance?" Wallace pleaded. "Perhaps his claws are too long. I could ask Dr. Grayson to clip them. Then could keep Bandit indoors except for the necessary, and then when he's out we … I … would keep watch on him." He tilted his head. "Please, Mrs. Wakefield, Aggie and I are so happy here. And you know yourself that there is no better house than this one."

Emma sighed. "Very well. But keep that cat away from the furniture and out of other guests' rooms."

"I will, I promise. Thank you!" He turned to his wife. "You see Aggie, it's all worked out. You don't have to give up Bandit."

Wondering if she'd just made a huge mistake, Emma made her way back down the stairs. Now she had to find fabric to replace the damage the cat had done. Deciding to ask Gibbs to move the chair to her parlor until the repair could be complete, she was startled as Mr. Thompson opened his door and stepped out.

"Oh, Mr. Thompson," she said, a bit breathlessly. "I'm sorry. I was so deep in thought I didn't see you for a moment."

"No more bad news, I pray."

"Not exactly, but wait," her eyes brightened and her smile returned. "You might be just the answer."

Thompson's brows drew together. "And to what might I be the answer?"

"Brocade."

"I beg your pardon?"

"Yes, that might well do it. Do you perhaps have a burgundy brocade?" At his blank stare, Emma rushed on. "Your samples," she said. "Do you have time to share them with me?"

"My samples?" He asked warily.

"Yes, the fabrics and trims you sell. I'd love to see them."

"Ah, those samples, I see." He rubbed his hand over his chin. "I'm afraid that won't be possible. You see they haven't arrived yet."

"Haven't arrived?" Now it was Emma's turn to look confused.

"Ah, yes, well there are too many for me to travel with so my office is sending them by post."

"Oh," Emma's shoulders sagged with disappointment. "But could you at least tell me if you carry any burgundy brocade?"

"Brocade?"

"Yes, the Milksop's cat has damaged one of the chairs in the parlor and I need to find brocade fabric to repair the damage."

"Well to be honest, Mrs. Wakefield, I'm not sure. The collection is extremely varied and I've no way of knowing if there is brocade in this shipment or not."

"But you will let me see the samples when they arrive?" Emma pressed.

"Certainly, but now I must beg my leave." And with a curt bow, Thompson turned and hurried down the walkway.

For a moment, Emma watched him go. How strange she thought. With the slightest encouragement, Bertram Hartwell, her other salesman, would launch into a recital of his products describing each in detail. Maybe Mr. Thompson was new to business, she thought. After all, he wore clothing more suited to gentry than to a merchant. With a shrug she turned her attention to finding Gibbs to get him to move the offending chair.

～

It was mid-afternoon the next day when Willie and Tobias met at the woodshed. The back of the shed, whitewashed and graced by a rose trellis, faced the house. The working side held stacked firewood, but it was half empty. A little farther off was a good sized pile of recently delivered un-split rounds.

Tobias called today's duty "attacking the pile." But it was not Tobias who attacked. Instead, he stood just behind the corner of the shed as a lookout.

Willie set a round on end and struck the far top edge of it with a light maul. Tobias had taught him well, and quite often the wood split on the first stroke. There were several wedges and a sledge hammer for the really stubborn pieces, but he rarely needed them. Every now and again Willie would take guard duty while Tobias stacked the cut wood in the shed. It was nearly dark by the time they'd finished.

"Still ain't got the whole shed full, Tobias," Willie observed.

Tobias nodded. "We'll be gettin' another load pretty soon. I'll see ya then?"

"Yes, sir." Willie, grinning widely, gave Tobias a mock salute and Tobias returned the gesture. Willie trotted off, making sure that the woodshed hid him from the house until he reached the trees.

There were many days when he wished that Tobias were his father. Or at least that his father was just like Tobias, hard working, fair, and most of all – sober. But it was a futile wish. As his father often said, "If wishes was horses, beggars would ride."

$\sim$

THE NEXT FEW days passed without incident. The Milksops kept a close eye on Bandit, and Emma decided rather than waiting for Mr. Thompson's samples to arrive she'd commission Mr. Bunting from the dry goods store to repair the damaged chair. She'd even managed to steal away and visit Clarissa several times and had been surprised to find that Mr. Thompson had been a huge help in cheering her friend.

When Clarissa's carriage arrived one afternoon, Emma was delighted to see her friend out and about. She was dressed in a black mourning gown with her curls still contained in a tight bun, but her face no longer held sorrow. Now she wore a steely determination.

"Clarissa," Emma said, hurrying down the stairs. "I didn't expect to see you today."

"I hope I'm not arriving at an inconvenient time, Emma," the girl's gaze darted from one end of the veranda to the other. "But I must speak with you immediately," she said in a hushed whisper. Emma started to lead her to the downstairs parlor but Clarissa reached for her arm. "Might we use your private parlor? I need to speak to you in private."

"Good afternoon, Miss Campbell," Gibbs said, as the pair reached the top of the stairs. "Will you be wanting tea, Mrs. Wakefield?"

"No thank you, Gibbs," Clarissa answered before Emma could reply. "I shan't be staying long." Turning, she started down the balcony to Emma's suite of rooms.

Emma exchanged a look with Gibbs that clearly said, "I don't have a clue." Then with a shrug she turned to follow her guest.

"Would you like to tell me what is going on?"she asked joining Clarissa in the parlor.

Clarissa paced from one end of the room to the other. "I hardly know where to begin," she said finally. "I'm so confused."

Emma sat and patted the space beside her on the sofa. "Come, sit and tell me what has put you in such a state."

Clarissa shook her head and continued to pace. "I'm not sure where the beginning is," she paused. "How well do you know Mr. Thompson?" she asked finally.

Surprised by the question, Emma could only stare. "I don't truly know him at all. He arrived last week and said Andrew had recommended Wakefield House should he ever be in St. Augustine and did I have a room to let. Why do you ask?"

Perching gingerly on the edge of the sofa, Clarissa sighed. "I just wondered what you knew of him, that's all."

"Has he done something improper?"

"Oh no," Clarissa said quickly. "He's been nothing but a gentleman. And I must admit he's truly helped to cheer me." She looked down at her clasped hands. "And listening to his stories of Andrew has greatly warmed my heart."

"Then what is wrong?"

Clarissa rose and began to pace again. "It's the stories," she said reluctantly. "All the stories he has of Andrew."

"I'm sorry, but I'm not following you."

Returning to the sofa, Clarissa sat again. "I've been so enamored with listening to the stories of my beloved that I don't think I was truly hearing what Mr. Thompson was saying."

Emma sighed. "Now I'm completely confused. You say the stories bring you peace but you've not been hearing? How is that possible?"

Clarissa's face clouded with worry. "That's just it. I'm not sure the stories Mr. Thompson has been telling are true. Having Andrew taken from me in such a horrible way, I've been desperate to cling to anything that would let me hold on a little longer."

Emma took Clarissa's clenched hands. "Darling, of course you want to hear about Andrew. That's natural. But what makes you think Mr. Thompson isn't being truthful?"

Clarissa's eyes filled with tears. "He told of an evening when he and Andrew went to an oyster festival to court some business acquaintances."

"Business acquaintances?" Emma said surprised. She knew that Andrew often worked undercover but something didn't sound right with this story.

"But don't you see," Clarissa wiped at a tear that traced

down her cheek, "Andrew was allergic to oysters. He never ate them."

"Oh...."

"So last night when I lay in bed recalling the stories, I couldn't help but wonder. If that story was wrong, what else was he telling me that wasn't truthful?"

"Dear, is it possible that you misunderstood what Mr. Thompson actually said? Or perhaps you thought he'd implied that Andrew had eaten the oysters when you knew that couldn't be true. If Andrew was working undercover and circumstances demanded he attend such a function, I'm sure he'd find something other than oysters to eat. Certainly that doesn't mean you can't take heart from the rest of Mr. Thompson's anecdotes. Some that I heard, after all, were quite humorous and at Mr. Thompson's own expense."

Clarissa sniffed and nodded. "You're right of course. I'm jumping to conclusions. And it's true, I have enjoyed spending time with Mr. Thompson. And I hated that I was starting to think ill of him, especially since he offered to take me sailing this afternoon."

"Sailing? Just the two of you?"

Clarissa rose. "Would you consider coming with us?"

"I wish I could, but right now..."

"I understand. I can probably get Jonathan to go along. He loves sailing as much as I do."

"That's your solution." Emma hugged Clarissa then walked her to the door.

But as Clarissa left, Emma had to wonder if she was doing her friend a favor by not expressing her own reservations about the man. His fabric samples had still not arrived and he didn't seem the least concerned over the matter. And oysters or not, would he really have joined Andrew at a business dinner? For a moment she wondered if he could have been working undercover with Andrew. That might explain the lack of samples. But if that was the case, why would he still be carrying on the charade? Was there something going on in St. Augustine that she wasn't aware of? Deciding that she needed to keep a better eye on Mr. Thompson, Emma returned to her chores.

CHAPTER 6

As she was coming from the dry goods store the next afternoon, Emma spotted Mr. Thompson entering the post office. Deciding to wait and see if his samples had arrived, she stood by the store's window and pretended to study the contents on display. In the reflection of the glass, she could clearly see the entrance to the post office; and moments later Thompson exited, empty-handed.

Emma frowned at herself in the glass as she watched him make his way down the street. If the man had nothing to show the merchants, how was he conducting his business? He left Wakefield House each afternoon after dinner and often didn't return until the evening meal was served. She had assumed he'd been visiting the local establishments making business contacts, but when she had mentioned his name to Mr. Bunting at the dry goods store, the man hadn't heard of Thompson.

Curious, Emma turned, and keeping a good distance between them, she began to follow him. It didn't take long for Thompson to reach his destination and Emma watched as he entered McConnell's Tavern.

Stunned, she actually stood for several minutes before she turned to make her way back home. Was Mr. Thompson spending his afternoons in the local tavern? He hadn't seemed like the sort to drink away the day and she'd never seen him act intoxicated. Still, how could a merchant support himself if he wasn't making any sales? Maybe he was an undercover agent like Andrew after all, and he was searching for some type of trouble that had to do with the tavern.

Wishing she had the answers, Emma slowly walked back home. If only there was someone she could ask. But in her mind, she could hear her James scolding her. "Your curiosity is going to get you into trouble, my dear." I know, she said to herself. I should just let it rest and forget about it. But as she made her way back home, she knew in her heart she wouldn't be able to let that happen.

EMMA WOKE SLOWLY from a deep sleep. Her eyelids fluttered. For a few seconds she remembered a little of what she had been dreaming, something about a chimney sweep getting too big and getting stuck in the chimney. Why one had such ridiculous dreams was a mystery - but what had woken her at such an early hour? She sat up, stretched, rubbed her eyes and wondered at the time when she heard a noise coming from the parlor. Frowning, she strained to hear. The sound came again - someone was talking, or muttering. But who would be up at this hour?

Rising she pulled on her dressing gown and went to peek through her chamber door. By the moonlight streaming through the windows, she could see a familiar form. Aunt Daisy. She was pacing back and forth in the parlor, her head lowered, her hands gesturing. She was clearly having a conversation, but she was alone.

Well, this was something new, even for Aunt Daisy. Talking to invisible beings was not her usual odd behavior.

Daisy was walking away as Emma approached her and tapped her on the shoulder. Daisy yelped as she spun around and Emma yelped in response. They both took a little hop back, their right hands to their hearts.

"What are you doing?" Aunt Daisy demanded.

"Me? Who are you talking to?" Emma countered.

Daisy looked around in confusion. "He was here a minute ago." She looked down and saw that her feet were bare and she had her night dress on. "Oh, good Lord."

"You must have been dreaming, and perhaps you were walking in your sleep. I have heard that people sometimes do that."

Daisy stiffened. "I was completely awake. And so was he."

"He?"

"Admiral Worthington."

Sighing, Emma steered Daisy into an overstuffed chair and glanced at the clock on the side table. "It's two o'clock, Auntie. Do you think you could ask the Admiral to visit at a more appropriate hour?"

"Emma dear, you wouldn't be so cavalier if you could see Admiral Worthington like I can."

"Perhaps not." Emma agreed, "but it looked like you were doing more than just seeing him. You were talking."

"We were, weren't we? Oh, I remember, he said something about the murder."

"His murder? But it was so long ago…" Emma could hardly believe she was having this conversation.

"Not his murder dear, Andrew's."

Emma rose abruptly. "Stop right this minute. We're not going to discuss murder at two in the morning."

"But dear," Daisy continued, not taking offense at Emma's tone, "someone has to solve Andrew's murder before his soul can rest in peace. And the Admiral very clearly said that we should pay attention to the cat."

"Aye!" Emma threw her arms in the air. "Go back to bed, Auntie. The authorities will solve the crime, not some long-dead seaman and his cat."

Daisy frowned but she let Emma lead her back to her room. "Bandit," she muttered as Emma turned to go. "I'm sure he meant Bandit."

Once again in her own bed, Emma had trouble sleeping. Were the authorities working to solve Andrew's murder? Again she wished there was someone she could contact for answers. Dare she send a telegram to his superiors at the Secret Service Agency and inquire about the progress of the investigation? She flopped over in her bed and pressed her face against the pillow. It might be a good idea she thought, if she had any clue as to who his superiors were. And what about Mr. Thompson? Could he also be an agent? He certainly wasn't playing the role of a merchant very well. Still arguing with herself about what to do next, Emma fell into a fitful sleep.

In the morning, Emma decided she must take some type of action. Deciding her hands were tied where Andrew's murder was concerned, she turned her attention to Mr. Thompson and his odd behavior. Determined to find out as much as she could about the man, she carefully composed telegrams to the officials he'd used as references. If everything was on the up-and-up, her inquiry would cause the man no problems, but if not, then she'd have some answers. As soon as the second seating of breakfast was complete, Emma made her way to the telegraph office.

She'd just stepped out when she saw Thompson exit the post office and again, the man was empty-handed. If he truly was waiting for fabric samples, she thought, he should be irate about the delay. She decided to follow him to see if his destination was McConnell's as before. But this time he surprised her by turning down St. George Street and walking in the opposite direction.

This made her task difficult, as this area of town was more residential. Near the end of the block she paused, knowing she could go no farther because if he turned around, he was sure to see her and she had no ready explanation for being there. Standing just behind a huge hawthorn bush, she watched him approach a house in desperate need of repair. But before he entered, he was joined by an unkempt individual who came from the side of the house. The men shook hands and Emma watched as the two went inside.

He must be an agent, she thought. Why else would he associate with someone from this part of town? Knowing she dare not stay and wait for him to leave, she turned and hurried back the way she came. Now rather than having any answers, she only had more questions. Hoping her telegrams would be answered in a timely manner, she told herself there was nothing more to do but wait.

~

AFTER THE NOONDAY MEAL, Emma was in the kitchen discussing the coming week's menu when Gibbs stepped into the open doorway. "Excuse me, Mrs. Wakefield, but Miss Clarissa's carriage has just pulled up out front."

Surprised, Emma stood and passed the list to Sadie.

"It's good she's getting out and about." Sadie took the list and slipped it into her pocket. "Would you like me to prepare some refreshments?"

"Let's wait a moment and see if she's planning to stay." Emma pulled off her apron. "I'll let Gibbs know if we need anything."

Emma rounded the corner as Clarissa reached the porch. "Clarissa, how nice of you to call."

"I had to. I had to thank you for suggesting that I go sailing with Mr. Thompson."

"I didn't suggest…" .

"My father was completely against the idea," Clarissa rushed on. "But when I told him you had suggested it, and that Jonathan would go along, he finally relented." She leaned closer. "If I had admitted that the suggestion had come from Mr. Thompson, it might not have been received quite so readily. But as you know, my father holds you in quite high regard."

"But I didn't …"

"So I need you to keep my confidence should the topic come up in conversation," Clarissa hooked her arm through Emma's and turned them toward the stairs. "I had such a wonderful afternoon I simply had to come and thank you. Actually, I would have called on you yesterday but my mother had invited friends for tea and you know…"

Once in Emma's parlor, Clarissa perched on the edge of the sofa. "Mr. Thompson was such a gentleman. He even produced a picnic basket for us to share. Although I wish he hadn't encouraged Jonathan to drink quite so much. I do believe my brother consumed an entire bottle of champagne. He was quite inebriated by the time we set out for home." She sighed. "But it was such a lovely afternoon."

Emma was torn. She was delighted to see Clarissa's smile back in place, but was not at all comfortable being part of such a deception. "I am glad you enjoyed yourself," she said hesitantly, "but you've put me in a very awkward position."

"Pish." Clarissa shook her head. "In a few days my father will completely forget about it."

"Still, I wish you…" Both women gave a start as the parlor

door eased open. But when the cat pranced in, Emma saw red. "I swear, that cat...."

"What's in his mouth this time?" Clarissa chuckled.

Emma stomped over to where Bandit had dropped his prize and now sat proudly washing his paw. "He's already ruined a chair in the downstairs parlor," she said, snatching up the sock. "And the Milksops promised they'd keep a better eye on him. If this is what they mean by a better eye then we're going to have some trouble." Emma turned to see all the color drain from Clarissa's face. "What..." she rushed to her friend and eased her back onto the sofa. "Clarissa what is wrong? What happened?"

"The sock," Clarissa's eyes filled with tears. "That looks just like Andrew's sock."

"What?"

Clarissa pulled the sock from Emma's hand. "This looks just like the sock I knitted for Andrew's birthday."

"You knitted a sock?" Emma tried to keep the skepticism from her voice.

Rubbing her finger over the diamond pattern, Clarissa looked up. "Remember when you helped me find cashmere wool?"

"Yes but..."

"And I borrowed your copy of the *Ladies' Journal*?"

"Yes, but..."

Clarissa continued to stroke the soft wool. "Well I never told you that the reason I wanted to borrow the magazine was because there was a pattern for knitting socks in that issue."

"But darling, you don't know how to knit."

Clarissa laughed and hiccuped at the same time. "I know. My first attempt was a disaster. But I so wanted to give Andrew something special for his birthday."

"But what makes you think this is Andrew's sock?"

"See," Clarissa let her finger trace over the pattern. "I made so many mistakes. The points of the diamond don't even line up correctly. At first I wasn't going to give them to him, but I'd worked so hard to complete them that...well I gave them to him anyway."

Emma could indeed see the mistakes in the pattern. "He must have been delighted to receive them," she said gently, knowing how difficult it would have been for Clarissa, who had no talent for knitting, to have accomplished such a task.

"He said he'd treasure them always." Clarissa looked up. "But how did the cat get one of Andrew's socks?"

Rising, Emma frowned. "I'm sure I checked that Andrew's door was locked after he left."

Clarissa rose as well. "Would I be asking too much for you to let me see Andrew's room? Perhaps he left some memento that I might have?"

"Of course. I don't know why I didn't think of that. I was going to wait to hear from his parents as to what they wished me to do with his possessions. But I'm sure they'd have no objection if you wished to keep something."

"Could we go now?"

The cat turned and darted out the door. "Don't think you're getting off so easily," Emma called after him. "I'll be dealing with you later."

The two made their way down the stairs to the veranda. "Andrew's room was here," Emma paused. Before she could pull out her keys, Bandit pranced out from the room next door with another sock in his mouth. He dropped the offering at Emma's feet then gave a loud MEOW.

"Come here you thief." The door swung completely open and Mr. Thompson stormed out clad in his trousers and shirt but with bare feet. Seeing the women he stopped abruptly. "I beg your pardon," he said hastily, "but that cat seems to have run off with my socks."

Emma picked up Bandit's prize and handed it back to Thompson. "Might I have its mate?" he extended his hand for the sock Clarissa still held.

"This one?"

"I must admit, Mrs. Wakefield, that I find this situation completely unsatisfactory." He all but snatched the sock from Clarissa's fingers.

"Those are your socks?" Clarissa's voice trembled.

"Ah, yes well…" Thompson hesitated, realizing he now held a pair of socks he'd taken from Andrew's bag. "Forgive my abrupt manner," he said with an expression of chagrin. "I didn't mean to be so rude."

"I hope the cat didn't damage them," Emma said quickly. "The wool is so soft, we were actually wondering where you might have purchased them."

Thompson winced. "They were not purchased at all," he admitted reluctantly. "My…my wife made them for me."

"Your wife?" Clarissa stammered. "You never said you were married…"

Thompson looked down again and struggled to find the right words. "My… my wife passed away a few months ago," he said quietly.

Her irritation vanishing as quickly as it had appeared, Clarissa took a step toward him. "Oh, I'm so sorry."

Thompson gave a shrug and looked up with an anguished expression. "My Rachel died in childbirth along with our son. It's not something I like to dwell on. I'm sure you understand."

"And she knitted the socks for you?" Emma asked.

He nodded. "She had many skills but she wasn't accomplished when it came to making clothing," he admitted reluctantly. He rubbed a finger over the soft wool. "She couldn't even get the points of the diamonds to line up properly. That's why I so treasure these."

"Of course you do," Clarissa said firmly. "Mr. Thompson I wonder if you'd do me the honor of dining with my family this evening."

"I'd be delighted," he responded, his flirtatious smile returning.

"Then since I have my carriage, shall I wait while you … ah… complete your wardrobe?"

Looking down at his bare feet, Thompson had the good grace to blush. "Please excuse me, ladies." Making a hasty retreat he returned to his room.

"I'm so pleased that's settled," Clarissa said, as she and Emma walked toward the carriage to wait. "And I must admit I feel terrible for thinking even for a moment that Mr. Thompson had Andrew's socks. That poor man. To have lost a wife and a child."

"He never gave any indication," Emma said quietly.

"Well of course not," Clarissa defended. "He's a true gentleman like my Andrew."

"Then I guess you'll want to come back at a later time to see Andrew's room?"

Now Clarissa paused. "I would like to see it today but," she hesitated as Mr. Thompson, now suitably dressed, left his room and moved to join them. "I'll come back tomorrow." She gave Emma a hug then let Thompson help her into the carriage. And with a wave they were off.

Emma watched the carriage make its way down the street. Something wasn't right. If Mr. Thompson was working with the Secret Service as an Agent like Andrew, because she was now completely convinced he wasn't a textile salesman, why was he spending so much time with Clarissa? He couldn't possibly believe Clarissa's family would be involved in a counterfeiting scheme. And why would he encourage her brother Jonathan to drink so heavily? And where had he purchased a picnic basket? Sadie hadn't prepared one for him or she would have mentioned it. She watched the carriage until it turned out of sight and hoped a response to her telegrams would arrive soon.

~

RACHEL THOMPSON SURVEYED the small boarding house room with disgust. "This is the best you have to offer?"

"For the price you are willing to pay," came the sarcastic reply from the prune-faced woman who had happily taken her money then proceeded to lead her to a third floor room the size of a closet. "You want a bigger room, you pay more."

Rachel forced a smile. "Then I shall make do with this. I do hope there is someone to bring me fresh water to wash?"

The older woman grunted as she turned to go. "I'll tell Francie. She does the fetch and carry on this floor. You want the water to be hot, pass her a coin or two. Otherwise wash with cold." And with that final declaration, the woman stepped out of the room and firmly closed the door.

Dropping her valise on the bed, Rachel took stock of her surroundings. A threadbare blanket covered the bed. A single chair stood next to a washstand with bowl but no pitcher, and a cracked mirror hung above.

When I find that no-good husband of mine I'm going to kill him, she thought. Giving a tired sigh, she removed her jacket and tried to shake off most of the traveling dust that she'd collected. She opened her valise and dug to the bottom to remove her purse, which was now bulging with the spoils of her recent carriage ride. She chuckled to herself. By the time her traveling companions realized that their wallets were quite a bit lighter, none would ever suspect that the demure doe-eyed lady who had traveled with them could have been the culprit. She counted her take then accessed the false bottom of her bag. Yes, her stash was growing quite nicely. She surveyed the room again. Certainly she could afford to stay in a nicer place; in fact, with this recent addition to her finances she could probably stay in the finest hotel in town. But until she located her husband, her instincts told her to lie low.

The knock at the door made her hastily close the hidden compartment of her bag and set it on the floor. Only then did she open the door.

"Sorry to disturb you, miss." The young girl, who looked to be no more than eight or nine, gave a short bob. "But the missus said you wanted water?"

"It's Mrs." Rachel said. "Mrs. Thompson. And you are?"

"Beg pardon, Mrs. Thompson." The girl bobbed again. "I'm Francie."

Rachel reached into her pocked and produced a coin. "Then Francie, do you think it would be possible to have some hot water so I might clean up after my journey?" She watched the girl's eyes grow wide at the size of the coin.

"Yes, missus, right away, missus, whatever you need, you just ask for me and I'll fetch it for you."

"Then let's start with some hot water, please." She handed the girl the coin. "And Francie, there will be more where that came from if you're speedy." Rachel smiled as the girl hurried to leave before she'd even finished speaking. Yes, she thought, moving to sit on the edge of the bed. She could make this work quite nicely.

Francie was as good at her word and returned with hot water much sooner than Rachel thought possible. And minutes later when the girl returned again with fresh towels that looked almost white and a pot of hot tea she hadn't even requested, Rachel knew she'd picked well.

"Tell me," she poured the tea while Francie hung just inside her door. "Have you been in the city long?"

Francie nodded. "Yes, ma'am. Been here long as I can remember."

"Then perhaps you could help me," Rachel paused and motioned for Francie to come farther into the room and close the door.

"Whatever you need missus," the girl said quickly. "You needs it and I can find it for you sure as you're sitting there."

"Well, this is delicate," Rachel said slowly. "You see, I need to find a person."

Francie frowned in confusion. "You want to find somebody?"

Rachel stirred her tea slowly as she decided on her story. She struggled to produce a tear before looking back up at the girl. "I need to find my brother." She let a tear run down her cheek. "Our mother is quite ill and the doctors have said there is no hope." Taking a hanky from her sleeve, Rachel dabbed delicately at her eyes.

"That's horrible." Francie took a step closer then paused, not knowing how to give comfort to someone so above her station.

"Yes, it is," Rachel sniffed. "The doctor said she has only a few weeks left and my mother's one desire is to see her first-born, my brother, again before she passes."

Francie wrung her hands together. "But how can I be of help, Missus?"

"Since I just arrived this day and I'm new to the city, I haven't a clue where to start looking for my dear brother."

Francie's brows drew together. "You could go to the post office," she said, brightening. "Mr. Wilson knows everyone in town 'cause they get their mail there."

Now Rachel frowned. "I know my brother is here, but I'm not sure it would be seemly for a lady like myself to inquire after a man. If you understand my meaning."

"But if you said you was asking for your brother and explained about your dying mom then…"

"Then the entire town would know my business and want to express their sympathy." Rachel looked down at her tea cup. "I don't think I could handle everyone knowing.…" She let her voice fade off and another tear slowly made its way down her cheek.

"I could go for you," Francie offered quickly. "If you told me your brother's name I could ask. No one would even have to know you was looking for him."

Rachel looked up, her eyes sparkling with hope. "Oh, could you really do that for me?"

Francie puffed out her flat chest. "I'd be happy to help."

"Oh, my dear," Rachel set down her tea cup and rose to stand before the girl. "You are such a godsend." She reached out and embraced the girl. "How can I ever thank you enough?" She reached into her pocket again and this time produced another coin. "You simply must let me pay you for such a kind service."

Francie beamed. Two coins in one day. She was going to be rich if this kept up. "I can be off as soon as you tell me the name." She gave another slight bob.

Rachel returned to her chair. "My brother's name is Samuel Thompson," she said quietly. "If you find him I wouldn't want you to approach him. After all, my news is so distressing."

Francie nodded, her excitement growing. "You just want to know where he's staying?"

"Yes. If you could locate him that would be wonderful. Then I can tell him about our mother. He's going to be so upset."

"I understand," Francie all but bounced in place, "and I'll find him for you."

"If you could," Rachel said as the girl turned to go, "I'd reward you for your efforts."

Francie just nodded and closed the door behind her. This was definitely her lucky day, she thought, carefully making her way down the stairs. She didn't even need to go to the post office. She already knew where Mr. Samuel Thompson was staying. Her dear friend Henny who worked at Wakefield House had been talking about him for days. Yes, she thought, I'll just wait awhile then go back and claim my reward. Surely my lucky day.

CHAPTER 7

*E*mma walked slowly as she made her way back from the market. Usually she enjoyed the trip, taking a moment here or there to speak with the various merchants as she passed. But today her thoughts were preoccupied. She was going to have to speak with Henny. Sadie, who worked harder than anyone Emma knew and who never had a bad word to say about anyone, had complained yet again. The girl kept disappearing before her chores were completed and was never on hand when Sadie needed her.

True, the girl had shown remarkable improvement with her own personal hygiene, keeping her hands and face washed and her hair tidy. And she was prompt every morning, and diligent in taking Mr. Thompson his breakfast tray, but as the day wore on her dedication to her chores faded. Now with her disappearing each afternoon and the suspicion Henny might be the culprit who took coins from her office, Emma knew she was going to have to let the girl go. It was only because Henny's family so desperately needed her income that she had given the girl the benefit of doubt. She couldn't prove Henny had taken the money and Aunt Daisy's missing bracelet had turned up. But now Sadie was at the end of her rope. Making the decision to tell Henny the next time she disappeared she would be terminated on the spot, Emma paused in front of Wakefield House as a carriage pulled up.

She watched as a small woman was assisted down. Her blond hair was artfully arranged and she wore a delicately knitted shawl over a burgundy dress.

"Good afternoon," Emma called, stepping forward. "May I help you?"

The woman took a moment to survey her surroundings before turning her attention to Emma. "I'm looking for the owner of the establishment. Can you direct me?"

Emma offered a smile. "I'm Mrs. Wakefield. Are you looking for accommodations?"

"No, I'm looking for my husband. Do you have a place where we might speak in private, Mrs. Wakefield?"

"That depends, who are you looking for?" Emma asked, realizing the woman carried no valise.

"I'm sorry, forgive me for being so abrupt. My name is Rachel Thompson. I've been led to believe my husband, Samuel Thompson, is staying here."

Emma worked hard to keep her surprise from showing. "Then I think we definitely need to speak in a more private setting, Mrs Thompson. Would you follow me?" She led the woman into the parlor on the first floor. "Would you like some tea?"

Rachel pulled off her gloves as she gazed about the room. She could certainly understand why Samuel had chosen to stay here. The furniture was highly polished and spoke of class while the faint scent of lemon hung in the air. "I'm afraid I'm not a tea drinker, but if coffee is available I'd love some."

"That can be arranged," Emma replied. "Give me a

moment." She met Gibbs, who was shrugging on his jacket just outside the door.

"I'm sorry, Mrs. Wakefield. I was in the kitchen when the carriage arrived."

"It's not a problem," Emma reassured. "But would you bring some coffee for my guest and tea for me please."

"I'll see to it immediately."

Emma stepped back into the parlor and found her guest had already made herself comfortable on the sofa. "We should have your coffee momentarily. Now, Mrs. Thompson, you said you were looking for your … husband?"

Rachel forced a smile that didn't reach her eyes. "I assume from your expression that my husband didn't let on that he was married." She shook her head and sighed. "I don't know why he does that. For some reason, when he goes off on a business trip, he seems to think he's better received if he doesn't mention he's married."

"I must admit I don't understand that logic," Emma wondered again if Thompson was indeed an agent working undercover.

"Because it isn't logical," Rachel replied. "But that is neither here nor there. What is important is that I find Mr. Thompson as soon as possible. You see, his mother has taken ill and according to the doctor has only a few weeks to live. She'll be devastated if her only son doesn't make it back in time."

The knock at the door made Rachel pause as Gibbs pushed the tea tray and positioned it before Emma.

"Thank you, Gibbs." Emma turned back to her guest. "I'm so sorry to learn that his mother is ill."

"Not just ill, she's dying. So I must find my husband and convey this information so he can return home with me as soon as possible. Will you instruct your man to tell him that I've arrived."

Emma studied the woman sitting next to her. On closer examination, she was much older than she'd first appeared. Her features were harder and something about her manner had Emma stiffening.

"I'd be happy to fetch Mr. Thompson for you but he's not here at the moment. You'd be welcome to wait until he returns, but I've no idea how long that might be. Might I ask where you and Mr. Thompson reside?"

"Mr. Thompson and I live in Charleston with our child."

"You have children?"

"Just one. Our son is going on nine months old."

"Charleston is a lovely city," Emma continued. "And I couldn't help admiring your shawl. Did you make it yourself?"

Rachel flipped the ends of the garment, which she'd secured in place with a brooch. "Surely you jest."

"It's quite a comely piece," Emma said. "And I know many young wives like yourself often enjoy knitting to make personal items like shawls or perhaps socks."

"Don't be ridiculous," Rachel scoffed. "I certainly don't knit socks. Mr. Thompson provides very well. If I wish to purchase something for my wardrobe I have abundant funds to do so."

"I didn't mean to give offense," Emma said tightly. "I simply wanted to compliment you on your taste. As I said, your shawl is quite lovely."

Rachel glanced down and smiled. "It is, isn't it. But tell me, are you sure you don't have a guess as to when my husband might return?"

"I'm sorry but no. I believe he was going to the Campbell's this afternoon and often he stays there to dine."

Rachel stood abruptly. "Then it's a waste of my time to sit here and wait for him. Do you have paper and pen that I might leave him a note?"

Emma rose as well and secured the necessary items from the rosewood desk in the corner. As she waited while the woman composed her note, she realized the silver sugar spoon no longer rested on the tea tray. She stiffened as Mrs. Thompson turned back to her and handed her a folded note.

"I trust you'll see that this gets to my husband's room."

Emma nodded. "I'll see to it personally."

"Then you may secure a carriage for me since I shan't be waiting here." And without waiting for Emma's response, the woman turned for the door.

Emma found Gibbs waiting on the other side.

"We need to arrange a carriage for Mrs. Thompson."

"That won't be necessary. Mrs. Thompson's carriage waited for her," Gibbs said formally.

"Oh good grief," Rachel sighed as she turned to go. "Now the man will want a fortune for his time."

Emma and Gibbs remained silent as they watched the driver assist the woman into the carriage.

"Well this puts things in a different light." Emma said finally.

"That's for certain."

But as Emma stood there watching the carriage start down the lane, she couldn't help wondering about the sock Bandit had produced. And why had Mr. Thompson told them his wife had died in childbirth? It was one thing to never mention a wife and let people assume what they would. It was quite another to tell a deliberate lie. And even if he was working undercover, what purpose would be served by a lie like that? She looked down at the note she still held and handed it to Gibbs.

"Would you put this in Mr. Thompson's room and then, if you can find Henny, tell her I need to speak with her. I'll be in my parlor. Oh, and Gibbs," she called as he turned to go, "don't be alarmed when you realize the silver sugar spoon isn't on the tea tray."

~

EMMA STOOD on the porch watching puffy clouds re-form themselves into the kind of shapes that children make a game of identifying. Her confrontation with Henny had been most unpleasant, and now thoughts of Andrew and her own beloved James kept running through her mind bringing the constant threat of tears. She wouldn't give in, she vowed, but she was so tired of being the strong one.

As if in answer to a prayer, a carriage stopped in front of Wakefield House and a sturdy, square-set man emerged. Without waiting for his luggage to be unloaded, he bounded up the steps and threw his arms around Emma.

"Oh, Howard," Emma cried, returning his strong embrace. "I'm so happy to see you!"

"Me too, dear cousin."

"But I'm so sorry about Andrew."

Howard released Emma and took a step back. "Let me pay the driver then you can tell me what you know about my brother's demise. My parents are a wreck as you can imagine, so I got few details from them."

Emma let out a sigh. "It's far more complicated than you might imagine. See to your driver then come inside."

A few moments later the two were in Emma's private parlor. Howard poured them each a finger of bourbon from a new bottle he had brought then took a seat beside her. "Now, what can you tell me?"

Emma looked down at the glass she held and once again fought back tears. "Who would have thought that our Andrew...."

"I know," Howard interrupted before taking a drink.

"Mother always said that I was the one who would come to a sticky end, being as quick with my fists as I am. Andrew was the one who always had his nose stuck in a book. Who would have thought that all that learning would make him want to become an agent with the Secret Service."

"But his death wasn't connected to his work. Jonathan told me the authorities in Tocoi thought it was a robbery gone bad. Perhaps the driver of the carriage?"

"That's what my parents believe." Howard gave her an appraising look. "But I know you, Emma dear, and of the three of us, you were always the clever one. There is something going on in that mind of yours, I can tell."

She shook her head. "I don't feel clever. Lately, all I feel is confused."

Howard reached over and covered her hand with his. "Then tell me."

Emma frowned. "I don't like to cast aspersions. If I'm wrong…"

"You have a suspicion. Tell me, Em."

"I have a boarder. He arrived the same day Andrew was to come. He said that he knew Andrew but some of the stories he tells of their acquaintance do not ring true. He claims to be in textiles but he has no samples. Then I thought he might be an agent like Andrew and working undercover. But…."

"You think he's lying?"

"Well, he certainly lied about being married."

"What?"

"Howard, this is so bizarre. Yesterday when Clarissa was here, Mr. Thompson told us his wife and child had passed. Then today a woman arrived and claimed to be his wife."

"Did you confront him about this?"

"Actually I haven't seen him since she was here." Emma looked down at her clenched hands then back up at

Howard. "I sent telegrams to the two references he provided when he asked for accommodations, but I haven't yet heard back."

"Well that's something. Did you contact the Agency?"

She shook her head. "I don't think they'd tell me one way or another. I was hoping they'd send someone to investigate but so far..."

"If they have started an investigation, then it's probably taking place in Atlanta as that's where he was working last."

"But according to Jonathan, Andrew was on his way home when it happened."

Howard rubbed a hand over his face. "I'm going to have to speak with Jonathan as soon as possible. Now, what do you want to do about this boarder? Do you want me to confront him?"

"No... but now that you're here, perhaps you could get close to him and find out what he's really about."

"I can do that. You said his name was Thompson?"

"Samuel Thompson."

"I'll see him at supper, then."

Emma shook her head. "He doesn't always take his evening meal here. In fact, he just sent word he'd be dining with the Campbells again."

Howard's eyes narrowed. "He's a friend of theirs?"

"No. When we heard of Andrew's death he accompanied me to the Campbells to pay his condolences. It wasn't until he started telling stories, anecdotes if you will, that things didn't ring true. Then with the dead wife showing up..."

Howard frowned. "I see why you would be suspicious. And if I find that Thompson had anything to do with my brother's death," Howard cracked the knuckles of his right hand. "He'll have me to answer for it."

"You will do no such thing, Howard Langley." She looked at him, half pleading and half threatening. "Promise me you'll not touch the man. Promise me that if we find he was somehow involved, you'll let the authorities handle it."

Howard inhaled deeply and looked about the room, hoping something would suddenly appear to get him out of this. At length he said, "All right, Emma, I promise." But if the man is responsible for my brother's death, he thought, there will be hell to pay, and I'll be the one extracting payment.

~

HENNY POUTED as she began to set the tables for supper. So she had taken a little time off. It wasn't like she hadn't come back. And where had Mr. Thompson been all afternoon? She'd spent ages in front of the mirror in Miss Daisy's bedroom fussing with her new scarf, but she'd finally found a way to wrap it around her shoulders which made her appear much older. She'd even used a bit of the old woman's lip dye. Then she'd walked the streets poking her head into various establishments but the man was nowhere to be found. She'd been hoping to accidentally bump into him again like she had two days before, and he'd buy her another ice cream. She didn't know which she'd enjoyed more, the delicious treat, or the fact that he'd purchased it for her. She just had to make him think of her as older and available, but today luck hadn't been with her. Then Mrs. Wakefield had been on a tear when she got back.

She set another plate on the table and sighed. So she was on probation, so what? If she played her cards right, soon she wouldn't even need this job. She caught sight of Gibbs in the doorway and started to move a little faster. The old goat would like nothing better than to report her, so she stuck out her tongue when he finally turned his back.

The table set, she picked up the meat platter and slowly made her way to the kitchen to see what horrible chore

Sadie wanted her to do next. If it was shelling more peas she was going to scream. She paused just outside the doorway when she heard Gibbs and Sadie speaking in hushed tones.

"Yes, she said she was Mr. Thompson's wife," Gibbs said quietly. "I don't know how Mrs. Wakefield managed to say so calm."

"Do you think she'll ask him to leave?" Sadie continued to stir the batter for a cake.

"I don't know what she'll do. He told her a lie plain and simple, and you know how she feels about lying."

At the sound of a dish crashing they both turned to find Henny standing in the doorway, the broken platter at her feet.

"Good grief, child!" Sadie set down the cake bowl and hurried over. "Are you hurt? Did you cut yourself?"

"I heard what you said," Henny stammered. "You said Mr. Thompson was married and that's not true."

"It is." Gibbs handed her a whisk and scoop to clear away the broken crockery. "I was there when his wife showed up. She's staying at Spruce House." His expression clearly showed his disdain.

"But Mr. Thompson said…"

"That's none of your concern," Sadie snapped. "You best be tending to your chores and not worrying about anything else. Mrs. Wakefield isn't going to be pleased when she finds her favorite meat platter is no more."

"But I thought…"

"And what's that hanging from your pocket?" Sadie took a step closer and gave the tail of Henny's scarf a good tug. The colorful silk scarf floated in the air between them.

"That's mine!" Henny cried, snatching the scarf back.

"And just what would you be doing with one of Miss Daisy's scarves?" Sadie challenged.

Henny felt her cheeks begin to burn. "She...ah...she gave it to me."

Sadie said nothing but simply continued to glare.

"She said she never used it anymore and I could have it for doing such a good job keeping her room tidy," Henny hurried on breathlessly. "You can even ask her."

"And don't think I won't," Sadie snapped. "Now get that platter cleaned up then get started on those potatoes, but for heaven's sake wash your hands first."

Henny managed to escape the kitchen before Mrs. Wakefield showed up to check on the meal's progress. She was going to be sacked, she thought as she moped behind the wood shed. Why, had she said Miss Daisy had given her the scarf? She should have told Sadie she'd purchased it herself or better yet that it belonged to her mother and she had permission to use it. Feeling like the world was crashing down on her, she rubbed at the tears that filled her eyes. Somehow she had to figure a way out of the situation. Maybe she could approach Miss Daisy and ask the woman if she could borrow the scarf. She was sure the old woman would say yes in fact, she probably didn't even remember that she owned the scarf. Or maybe if she was questioned she could convince Mrs. Wakefield the old woman had actually given her the scarf. It wasn't as if Mrs. Wakefield didn't know how forgetful Miss Daisy had become. Yes, she thought, giving a huge sniff, she'd simply tell Mrs. Wakefield that Miss Daisy had given her the scarf. After all it would be her word against that of an old woman who couldn't remember anything these days.

Feeling more confident, she pulled the scarf from her pocket and ran the soft fabric through her fingers. But what was she going to do about Mr. Thompson? Was his wife beautiful? She'd need to go to Spruce House and see for herself. Carefully she rolled the scarf back into a ball and tucked it deeper in the pocket of her skirt, under her apron this time. Yes, she'd go to Spruce House and with any luck her friend Francie could tell her what was really going on.

$\approx$

RACHEL RETURNED to her room and found Francie loitering on the balcony just outside her door.

"Francie, be a dear and get me a pot of coffee."

Francie gave a short bob and darted off.

Unlocking the door to her room, Rachel entered and began to remove her purchases. Knowing Francie would be quick hoping for another coin or two, she hastily re-wrapped the box of confections and secured a note on the top. She was sitting in her chair by the window when Francie returned with a ceramic pot and a china cup and saucer.

"I had the cook fix the pot just like you like it," she said, carefully setting them on the small end table. "Sugar but no cream."

"You are such a dear," Rachel said slipping the girl another coin. "What would I do without you?"

Francie beamed with pleasure.

"Do you think you might have time to do an errand for me?" she asked, sipping her coffee.

"I'd try my best, missus."

"Well, you did so well in finding my brother I'm sure you could manage this. I need you to deliver a package to Wakefield House for me."

"You want me to take something to your brother?" Now Francie frowned in confusion. "But I thought you went to tell him about your mum being ill?"

"I had planned to, but when I arrived at Wakefield House, he was out for the afternoon and they didn't know when he might return. I was told he was visiting with a family named Campbells. Do you know the name?"

Francie gave a snorting laugh. "Everyone in St. Augustine knows that name. They be the richest folks in town."

"Really…" Rachel drawled out the word.

Francie nodded. "They have that grand house on King Street. You can't miss it. Do you want me to take your package there?"

"Oh no," Rachel sat up straighter in her chair. "No, that won't be necessary. I'd just like you to take it to Wakefield House and ask them to put it in his room for when he returns. Could you do that?" As she spoke, Rachel pulled a small handful of coins from her pocket.

Francie's eyes grew wide with excitement. If this kept up she'd have enough to purchase a new pair of shoes since the ones she was wearing were already worn through on the bottom. "I can take that right now if you wish."

Rachel handed over the package. "Now scoot so I can get some rest before it's time to dine." Rachel waited until Francie was out the door and she heard the girl's clomping footsteps fade away. Then she stood and began to pace. How dare he do this to her, she fumed. Spending the afternoon with the richest family in town. Well if he thought he could cheat her out of what was sure to be a profitable scam, he'd learn soon enough that she wasn't someone to be trifled with. And she knew just how to bring him back to her side, begging for her forgiveness.

Rachel had barely finished her coffee when another knock sounded at her door. Knowing it wasn't Francie's hesitant tap-tap, she rose slowly and crossed the small room. "Who's there?"

"Open the damn door, daughter," came an angry male voice.

Rachel sighed with frustration as she pulled open the

door to admit her father and brother. "What are you two doing here?" she demanded.

"The bigger question is what are you doing here?" Arnold Smith towered over his petite daughter. "You gave the babe to your ma and then disappeared without a word."

Refusing to be cowed, Rachel crossed her arms over her chest and glared back defiantly. "I'm here to find that no-good husband of mine and make him come home."

"You're a fool, girl. The man is a scoundrel through and through. Cut your losses and come home now."

Rachel turned her back on her father. "I'll do no such thing. He thinks he can desert me and take up with some rich society family? Well he can just think again."

Scott Smith, tall and thin where his sister was petite and curvy, leaned insolently against the open door jam. "And just how do you propose to get him to come back home when you couldn't keep him there in the first place?"

"Oh, I'll get him back," she lifted her chin and glared at her brother. "I've already found out where he is staying."

Scott straightened and stepped farther into the room, closing the door behind him. "You really want the bastard back?"

"He's my husband and the father of my child. And I'll not sit idly by while he gallivants up and down the coast trying for another score."

"Ah, there's the rub of it, daughter," Arnold said with a gleam in his eye. "He's found a rich mark and has no plans to share."

"And if he thinks he can do me out of whatever would be my take, he's mistaken," Rachel sat again on the room's single chair.

"So how do you want to work things?" Scott asked, taking a seat on the edge of the bed.

"I don't want you two to do anything except disappear. I've already put my plan into motion."

Scott pounded a fist into his open palm. "Surely you don't mean to deny me a little fun."

Rachel only grinned. "If your fist happens to find a suitable face to rearrange I'll never object. The man needs to be taught a lesson if he thinks he can cheat me out of my share of a good score."

CHAPTER 8

*S*amuel Thompson sat alone at a table at McConnell's. None of his gambling pals had yet appeared. He leaned with his back against the wall, beer in hand, and surveyed the scene. There were seven people at the bar, all of them working folks. He hadn't seen any gentlemen the other times he'd been in either. All the better for him, he knew. It was far easier to relieve these men of their money than the more sophisticated gentry. It hadn't been so difficult with Andrew Langley though, perhaps because he was so besotted with his fiancée.

Samuel smiled to himself. Thanks to Langley, he had captured the attention of the city's wealthiest family. Clarissa Campbell would be his soon enough, he reckoned. All he had to do was soothe her while she mourned poor Andrew. It was simply a matter of time before she fell under his spell. The father and the brother, however, were not so easily pleased. But tonight he had a plan. He had enough in his pocket to switch to the high stakes table and with skill, he'd collect enough to make a generous donation to the Campbell's favorite charity. That was bound to put him in better graces with the father. The brother was another problem, but he was confident that he'd think of something. Between that and the other venture he had in the works, things were moving along quite nicely.

From his accustomed seat he could still see the door quite clearly. Jonathan Campbell, Clarissa's brother, was the first to enter. Jonathan spied Samuel and walked toward his table. Samuel rose and shook the man's hand, motioning him to have a seat. He signaled the barkeep to bring a pitcher of beer.

"I figured you might be here," Jonathan said.

"And I'm quite surprised to see you, but glad for your company," Thompson replied.

The barman approached and placed a pitcher and a second glass on the table.

"I'd prefer a glass of port," Jonathan spoke to the barman.

Samuel waited until Jonathan had his drink. "What's on your mind?"

"I want to know what kind of designs you have on my sister."

"Designs? On a grieving woman? Surely you must think me six kinds of a cad."

Jonathan remained silent.

"Well, I cannot really blame you. Except for the afternoon we spent sailing, you don't know me at all." He set his glass down even as Jonathan picked his up. "It's true, I cannot help but have feelings for Clarissa, of which I hope she is not aware, as it is unseemly given the circumstances…"

His narrative was interrupted by the appearance of Mac, the establishment's owner. He looked down at Samuel. "The boys are gathering in the back but haven't started yet. They want to recoup some of what you took off them last time."

"They can try but they'll be at the wrong table. I'm raising the stakes tonight."

Mac grunted. "Can't say I'm surprised. This evening I'll be joining you."

"Really? I've never seen you play. I believe I was told you didn't."

"I do, when I have reason. You planning to join us Campbell?"

Jonathan grinned. "Wouldn't miss it."

Samuel picked up his beer and moved to the back room, followed by Mac and Jonathan.

The room held two round wooden tables. Each had space for six players. One table had a limit, the other did not. Samuel, who usually played at the limit table, headed toward the high stakes one.

Frank Jefferson nursed his beer and glared at Samuel. "You'll be playing with my money tonight, Thompson," he grumbled. "Ain't ya gonna give me a chance to get it back?"

"Not tonight," Samuel took a seat by the far wall. "Unless you want to join us over here."

There was a lot of grumbling coming from the other table, but Samuel ignored it. Mac took the seat next to him while Jonathan sat across the table. Before the first hand could be dealt Howard Langley strode into the room.

"Langley!" Mac rose to shake the man's hand. "How good to see you. But sorry for your loss."

Jonathan stood as well and embraced Howard with a one armed hug. "When did you get into town?"

"Just arrived. Am I too late to get into the game?"

"No, we were just starting," Mac said. "Let me introduce you to Thompson."

Samuel stood and reached across the table to shake Howard's hand. "Samuel Thompson here. Langley...were you related to Andrew Langley?"

"Brother," Howard's expression never changed as he took

the empty seat next to Jonathan. "We playing or talking all night?"

"Let's get started." Mac passed the cards to Samuel. "Your deal."

It took Samuel awhile to get into the rhythm of the table, especially with Jonathan and Howard Langley there. Still he did well, raising the stakes yet not winning too much on hands he dealt. By the time he'd dealt six hands he was chatting away, once again totally comfortable with himself and his skill.

Thompson was half way through his seventh deal when Mac slammed down on his wrist just as he was about to drop a card into his own pile. "King of diamonds." Mac said tersely.

"Let go of my wrist," Samuel demanded.

"Not until you let go of that king." Mac banged Samuel's hand on the table and the card fell out, face down.

"You gonna tell me that's not the king of diamonds?"

"How would I know what it is? You're the one who cut the deck."

"Every deal you force my cut. I've seen you do it. Then you deal yourself cards from the bottom."

The men at Samuel's table stared at him. Howard reached across the table and flipped over the card. It was the king of diamonds.

Samuel could hear the muttering of players at the other table. A chair scraped and an instant later Frank Jefferson was on his feet.

"You fookin' bastard! Yer a liar and a cheat and I want my money back."

"We'll all have our money, ya blackguard," another voice boomed.

Mac rose and spread out his arms. "Easy, lads, it will all come back to you. No need for violence. Thompson is going to empty his pockets right here on the table. Then he's going to let himself out the back door and never be seen here again. Isn't that right, Thompson?"

Quietly a tall, thin man stepped through the door from the bar and closed it carefully behind him. Seeing the intruder, Samuel stood.

"Thompson?" Mac turned back to face him.

Before Samuel could answer the stranger stepped forward.

"You bloody waste o' flesh," the man spit. "You reckon you can just walk out on your wife and child?"

At this, Jonathan Campbell rose as well. "Wife? Child?"

"Aye. He's been married to my sister these last three years. Though for the life of me I can't see what she wants with him."

"Really?" Jonathan turned back to Samuel. "This is true?"

Samuel nodded. He was outnumbered by far but it was his brother-in-law Scott whose wrath he feared the most, so he was taken by surprise when it was Jonathan who sprang forward and reached over the table. He grabbed Samuel by his shirt and pulled him across the table, dropping him on the floor in the middle of the room.

"You dare toy with my sister's emotions, you bastard. I'll beat some sense into you, I swear!"

Wasting no time, Frank Jefferson jumped on the pair and the others happily joined in the fray. Kicks and punches went flying for several minutes when the room suddenly went dark.

"What the hell?"

"Take it easy." Mac cautiously made his way to the door. As he opened it, light spilled in from the bar. Patrons in the back room dusted themselves off as Mac retrieved some matches and re-lit the candles that had so mysteriously gone out.

Frank looked around. "The bastard's gone!" Curses filled the air as the group realized that both Samuel Thompson and Howard Langley had indeed disappeared.

Mac walked to the open window. "And here's how they did it. I thought I felt a chill just before Mr. Campbell got hold of him. Breeze must have come through and blown out the candles."

"But why did Langley follow him out? He didn't lose any money to the cheating bastard." Frank's spittle did not quite reach the spittoon in the corner. "Thompson's got ta be the luckiest bastard in the world."

"Luck ain't nothin' against knives and fists," another threatened. There were "Ayes" all around.

"Settle down," Mac called over the voices

"What's that?" All eyes turned toward the table where Thompson had been sitting. A drink had overturned, running onto some of the bills still resting on the table.

Mac walked over and picked up the soggy paper only to watch the ink on the bill run into an unreadable smear.

"It's a counterfeit!" Frank cried. "Besides being a cheat the man was playing with counterfeit money." Other voices joined with Frank's cry of outrage.

"Settle down," Mac demanded. "I'll take this up with the authorities first thing in the morning. But right now everyone needs to calm down. Straighten those upturned chairs and I'll fetch a few pitchers... on the house."

"And what about our money?" Frank demanded. "Langley can mess with Thompson all he wants but I want my money back."

As the grumbles continued, Scott motioned to Jonathan Campbell to follow him out the back door.

The two men walked a full block before speaking. Scott assessed the value of his companion's clothes, now a bit worse for wear. "You're a gentleman?"

"Guilty."

"That your first fight?"

"It was." Jonathan used his sleeve to wipe blood from his lip and looked over at Scott with a grin. "But, my God, it was fun." Then his smile vanished. "But I ought to have killed the bastard. Maybe I still will."

Scott extended his hand. "Scott Smith, the bastard's brother-in-law."

"Jonathan Campbell. The man who wants to see the bastard gone."

Scott thought a moment then gave Jonathan an appraising look. "You know, I think I have a way we can get him. You game?"

Jonathan nodded.

"Then come with me and we won't have our bruises be for naught."

⁓

Samuel climbed the stairs to Rachel's room at Spruce House. It had been pure luck he'd managed to elude Howard Langley. Now every bone in his body ached. He wanted answers from his wife and he wanted them now. What had she been thinking to show up like this?

He found room 22 without trouble and knocked on the door. There was no answer.

A young girl, from her clothing quite clearly a servant, called out to him from the end of the balcony. "Are you wanting someone, good sir?"

"Mrs. Thompson, she's not answering."

"You're Mrs. Thompson's brother, then?"

"Brother?" He hesitated, then nodded as the young girl stepped closer.

"Mrs. Thompson's gone out for a stroll with yer father. It's such a lovely evening and there's a full moon."

"I see." He hesitated again. He hadn't known his father-in-law was here too. "Perhaps you would be so kind as to let me in so that I may wait for her?" It was more command than question, but the girl seemed eager to please.

"Of course. I'm sure Mrs. Thompson wouldn't want you waiting out here on the balcony." She produced a key ring from her apron pocket and opened the door for him. "My name is Francie. Let me know if you need anything."

Samuel stepped into the room and with the light from the moon quickly found the side table with candles and matches. He lit a candle then surveyed his surroundings with disgust. What scheme was his dear wife hoping to play by staying in a flop like this?

His anger grew by the minute as he paced the length of the tiny room and back. By showing up this way she had completely ruined all the preparations he had made to lure Clarissa, and her money, his way. And now with that part of his cover blown, there was the danger that his other operation would not be able to get off the ground either. He rolled his shoulders and winced at the pain. Someone was going to pay dearly for ruining his plans. But in his current condition, he'd have to wait to take on his wife, especially since her brother and father were around. No, he'd find a way to get even, but for now….

He was about to leave when he noticed a bottle of wine on the bedside table. He'd have preferred a bottle of whiskey but this would have to do. Taking the bottle he extinguished the candle, and left. He'd be back as soon as he figured out exactly what he should do about Rachel and her obnoxious brother.

Samuel headed toward the sea. There was nothing like a

bottle of wine and the sound of the surf to clear a man's head. And the way his head ached, it could do with clearing.

～

STANDING in the open doorway to the kitchen, Emma frowned as she watched Henny leave Mr. Thompson's room with his breakfast tray. Checking her watch she was even more confused. The man had never completed his breakfast so early.

"He's not there," Henny sniffed as she approached Emma. "Mr. Thompson is gone." The girl's eyes filled with tears. "I could tell his bed hadn't been slept in and he's not here to break the fast. He's gone and he never even told me good-bye."

Emma stepped aside so Henny could carry the tray into the kitchen. "I'm sure Mr. Thompson has not left for good," Emma said, wondering if after the appearance of his wife the man had indeed departed.

"But why didn't he say good-bye to me?" Henny wailed as tears coursed down her cheeks.

"And what makes you think a gentleman like himself would be needing to tell his maid his business?" Sadie wiped her hands on a dish towel then took the coffee pot from the tray. "You be forgetting your place girl, and that's a fact."

"But he was so nice to me…."

"Don't mistake politeness for more than it was, Henny," Emma said, watching the girl wipe her tears with the sleeve of her blouse. "Since you're not needed to attend Mr. Thompson, start upstairs and see if Mrs. Acosta needs anything."

"But…" at the look on Emma's face, Henny fell silent. Hanging her head, she turned and walked away.

"Something's up with that one," Sadie said. "She's been

mooning over someone and now I think we have a good idea of who it is."

"I'm not pleased with any of this," Emma said. "And after learning that Mr. Thompson is married when he clearly told Clarissa and me that his wife and child had died, I don't think I want him to continue to stay here."

"Do you think that's why he didn't appear for supper last night? He knows something is amiss."

"Well, someone is lying," Emma said. "I'm just not sure who."

Sadie turned back to her cake batter. "Maybe Mr. Thompson was called away unexpectedly and left you a note in his room. He might not even know his wife arrived. If she is his wife, that is."

"If he left a note Henny would have seen it and brought it to me."

Sadie shook her head. "I'm thinking the girl can't read. You'd best be checking that room for yourself to see what's what."

Emma sighed. "You're right of course. I'll see to it after breakfast."

IT WAS mid-afternoon before Emma had a break in her routine that allowed a moment to check Mr. Thompson's room. He hadn't appeared for their noonday meal and now she was truly concerned since Howard hadn't appeared either. Using her keys she let herself into Howard's room first and could see that the bed hadn't been slept in. Some of his clothing had been tossed haphazardly on a chair, but she knew Howard had never been concerned with neatness. Carefully locking his door, she moved to Mr. Thompson's room.

Here the room was tidy and a quick check of the wardrobe told her that Mr. Thompson meant to return as it still contained his clothing. But as Henny had reported, his bed hadn't been slept in. Emma began to wonder if he was simply too ashamed to face her, knowing he lied about his family.

Emma stepped to the desk and found a box of sweets with a folded note resting on the top. Picking up the note she quickly scanned the contents. A gift from his wife that told him where she was staying. Carefully, Emma refolded the note and set it back on the package. That was the answer, she thought. Mr. Thompson had returned and finding the note had gone to see his wife. Had he stayed the night with her? And what reason could he possibly present to excuse the lies he'd told? Deciding to advise him that he was no longer welcome to continue his stay, Emma turned to see Bandit dart into the room.

"Oh no you don't," she told the cat. "Out of here now!"

The cat, ignoring her completely, raced to the far side of the bed and started batting at two cords that hung down from under the edge of the mattress.

"You're not going to ruin another thing in this house," Emma said, making a shooing noise toward the cat. But Bandit was not to be denied his plaything and grabbing one of the cords in his mouth, continued to tug.

Emma caught him with one hand as she knelt down beside the bed to assess the damage. "Let go of that you thief."

The cat gave a loud meow then wiggled away and fled through the open door.

Emma heaved a sigh and turned back toward the bed. Frowning, she examined the cords that the cat had tugged. They didn't belong to the mattress or the underpinnings. Giving them a tug herself, she was stunned when a soft cloth bag appeared from under the mattress. Why had Mr. Thompson felt the need to hide his personal property? Did he believe that Henny was not trustworthy when she was in his room alone?

For several moments Emma considered what to do. She should just tuck this back under the mattress. But hadn't James always said her curiosity would always get the best of her? She weighed the bag in her hand, then unable to resist, pulled the cords to open the pouch. Emma's breath caught in her throat and she stared in horror as the contents spilled into her hand.

CHAPTER 9

*E*mma paced from one end of her parlor to the other. She had sent a message asking Clarissa to attend her at her earliest convenience. What if she was wrong, she thought. But dear God, she knew she was right. Even though she was expecting it, the tap on her parlor door made her jump. Gibbs eased open the door. "A telegram just arrived, Mrs. Wakefield." He stepped farther into the room and handed her the folded note.

Emma's eyes grew wide as she read the angry response to her earlier inquiry. *Mayor Wheaton of Savannah has never heard of Samuel Thompson and is quite put out the man has used his good name as a reference.*

She looked back at Gibbs. "If Mr. Thompson should return to his rooms, please notify me immediately then go for the authorities."

"Madam?"

"The man is a fraud and I have reason to believe that is not the worst of it."

Gibbs nodded. "Should I fetch the authorities now?"

"No," she took a breath to steady her nerves. "Let me wait

until Clarissa confirms what I already know. Then I'll ask you to fetch Captain Delgado from the fort. He'll know best how to handle the situation."

"As you wish. If you'll excuse me, I believe I hear Miss Clarissa's carriage now."

Moments later Clarissa entered the room and her expression of total fury took Emma by surprise. Had she guessed what Emma was about to show her?

"Did you know?" Clarissa challenged. "Did you know the cad was married?"

Emma blinked. "How did you find out?"

Clarissa waved her arms in the air. "My brother and Howard got into a fight with the bastard last night at McConnell's. Seems Mr. Thompson's brother-in-law showed up and all hell broke loose."

"Are they all right?" Emma gasped. "Howard never came back last night and he wasn't here for either breakfast or dinner."

Clarissa shrugged. "I can't speak for Howard, but Jonathan never came home last night either. This morning he appeared at breakfast with a swollen split lip. But he was in fine spirits so he's not my concern at the moment. And I haven't seen Howard since he came to the house last night asking for my brother. Now tell me, did you know?"

Emma shook her head. "Not until Mr. Thompson's wife showed up yesterday afternoon asking to see him."

"The wife he told us had passed away with the death of his child?" Clarissa asked sarcastically.

"That would be the one."

Clarissa flopped down on the sofa. "But why would he do that? I simply don't understand what the man thought to gain by lying about the existence of a family."

Emma took a deep breath. "I haven't a clue to his reasoning, but I fear I have something more distressing to share with you."

Clarissa simply rolled her eyes. "Could anything be more surprising? I think not."

"Don't be too sure," Emma said quietly, reaching for the cloth bag that rested on the end table. "Would you look at these and tell me if you recognize them."

"What have you got there?"

The color drained from Clarissa's face as Emma emptied the contents of the bag into her lap.

Clarissa's hand trembled as she picked up the gold pocket watch. Her eyes closed as she brought the watch up to press against her heart.

"It's Andrew's?"

Clarissa could only nod. "Thank you," she finally opened her eyes. "This means more to me than you could ever know." She smiled down at the watch then gently opened it. "It belonged to Andrew's great-grandfather and his father passed it on to him on his sixteenth birthday." Then she frowned and looked back up at Emma. "But I don't understand why Andrew would leave this behind? I know for a fact it was one of his most cherished possessions."

"And these?" Emma gestured to the gold ring and tie clasp she still held.

"Those belong to Andrew too," Clarissa reached for the ring. "But why would he leave all this behind when he left for his trip? He never gave me any indication that his business was dangerous. Do you think he had a fear of being robbed?"

"I didn't find these in Andrew's room," Emma said, feeling her anger start anew now that her suspicions had been confirmed. "In fact, I've not been in Andrew's room since he left."

"I don't understand," Clarissa frowned. "Then how… where..?"

"They were in Mr. Thompson's possession."

"What!"

"Mr. Thompson never came back last night," Emma hurried on, "and when he didn't show for either breakfast or dinner today, I decided to check his room. The Milksop's cat raced in, and before I could catch the creature, he'd pulled these cords from beneath the edge of the mattress."

"Mr. Thompson had Andrew's watch hidden under his mattress?"

Emma could only nod. "Andrew's watch and ring, and other pieces of jewelry I didn't recognize."

Clarissa's eyes grew wide. "Does this mean what I think it means?"

Emma took a deep breath. "I fear Mr. Thompson might have been the one who caused Andrew's death. I can come to no other conclusion with these items in his possession. And today I received a telegram from the mayor of Savannah. Mr. Thompson's references were forged. The mayor had no idea who Thompson was and indeed was quite put out to hear someone was using his good name without permission."

"And for the past few days the man has been deceiving us all and trying to get into our good graces? I'm going to kill the bastard," Clarissa spat angrily. "Night before last he tried to talk my father into investing in some new venture."

"Oh no."

Clarissa shook her head. "Daddy wasn't as gullible as I apparently am," she said angrily. "So what shall we do?"

"Now that you've confirmed my worst suspicions, I'm going to ask Gibbs to send for Captain Delgado at the fort. He resides here and I believe he's currently assisting the town marshal. We can give him this information and he'll know what to do."

Clarissa stood and began to pace. "I can't believe I sat and listened to all those stories believing they were true."

~

IT DIDN'T TAKE LONG for Captain Delgado to arrive. He listened patiently as Clarissa explained how Thompson had told them his wife and child were dead, then Emma showed him the jewelry she found in Mr. Thompson's room.

"That's Andrew's jewelry," Clarissa said angrily. "And the socks. Damn it, those were the socks I made for Andrew."

"Socks?"

"The Milksop's cat has a habit of stealing socks," Emma started to explain.

"Ah, yes, Bandit," the Captain grinned. "I'm all too familiar with that little monster."

"He stole a sock from Mr. Thompson's room. I recognized it as one I had made for Andrew. But then Mr. Thompson said his wife made it for him."

"His dead wife," Emma added.

"His dead wife knitted a sock?"

Clarissa shook her head. "No, he lied about that."

"She showed up yesterday," Emma added.

"The dead wife?"

"The wife who is very much alive," Emma continued. "Mrs. Thompson didn't seem at all surprised that her husband had indicated he wasn't married. She even went on to explain he often did that when he traveled on business."

"The cad," Clarissa added.

"But he didn't come back to his room last night or show up for meals today."

"I did notice his absence," the Captain said slowly. "But I thought he was in his room nursing his ego."

"What?" Clarissa and Emma both spoke at once.

"There was quite a ruckus at McConnell's last night."

"Oh, I know about that," Clarissa added suddenly. "My brother evidently played a part. Seems Mr. Thompson's brother-in-law showed up and ... well you probably know the rest."

The Captain nodded. "And now we know that besides being a cheat at cards, the man is quite probably a murderer as well." He turned to Emma. "Have you seen Mr. Langley? He was also at McConnell's last night."

"I checked Howard's room just a while ago. He never came home last night and I haven't seen him today." She clasped her hands tightly in her lap. "What should we do now?"

"Absolutely nothing," Captain Delgado moved to the door. "I'll have my men assist the police in starting an immediate search. If Thompson does show up, do not confront him. Instruct Gibbs to contact me or the police as discreetly as possible."

"My father is already out looking for him," Clarissa pressed a hand to her chest. "He was furious when my brother didn't come home last night. Then at breakfast this morning Jonathan told us that Thompson was married."

"If I find your father, Miss Campbell, I shall send him home. You'd do best to return there yourself. Thank you for your assistance ladies."

"We can't just sit here and do nothing," Emma complained.

"Then reward that damned cat with a bowl of cream." And with that, Captain Delgado turned and left.

"I can't go home," Clarissa said when they were alone again. "I'd go crazy wondering what was happening. Let's take a walk. But not into town. I wouldn't relish bumping into Mr. Thompson knowing what we do."

"The sea wall," Emma said. "We certainly can't get into any trouble there. Let's get out of here and get some fresh air. Just let me tell Gibbs then we can be off."

∼

WILLIE WAS WALKING past the Donodan house when he stopped abruptly. Two workmen were busy tearing down the garden wall which separated the house's yard from the vacant lot next door. He had heard that the Donodans had bought the lot, but it never entered his mind that it would cause him trouble. At the moment the men worked on the far end of the wall, but Willie realized it wouldn't be long before they reached the near end and discovered the secret hiding place he and Pete had created all those years ago: the spot where he'd hidden his pouch of coins. What to do? He needed to get his stash, and he needed to do it now.

The workmen were about half-way down the six foot tall wall, on the side of the vacant lot. From the looks of things, they would have the whole wall down before tomorrow. His hiding place was on the house side. He had to take the chance if he wanted to retrieve his money.

The house was owned by the family of his former school friend, Pete Donodan. Willie decided that if he were caught he would just tell the truth: that he had been hiding his coins so that his father could not get to them. Everyone knew how his father was. They would understand, he hoped. Still he really did not want to be caught. He stopped at the gate and gave a quick glance at the house. The place seemed pretty quiet. He sprinted across the lawn and crawled behind the hedge that grew next to the wall. Feeling safe now, he removed the loose rocks he and Pete had found when they were little, before his dad had started drinking and before Pete got himself kicked to death by a crazed horse. Willie thought about Pete every time he came to the wall, about how they used to hide notes to each other. But now the wall was coming down. Gone. Just like Pete.

He pulled out the pouch, stuffed it in his pocket, and for

no good reason replaced the rocks. He rubbed them with the knuckle of his index finger, like you would rub the chin of a cat. He was saying a final goodbye to Pete.

Half an hour later, walking aimlessly, he was still thinking about Pete, wondering if they'd still be friends had Pete lived, wishing he could go back in time and tell Pete to stay out of that stall.

Willie had ambled as far as the pharmacy when a hand gripped his arm.

"Hey boy, where ya goin'?" His dad looked down at Willie's bulging pocket. "And what ya got there, rocks?" He fingered the pocket and the coins clinked. "My God, boy, where'd ya get such loot?" His father tried to dig into the pocket but Willie pushed the hand away. His dad grabbed him by the neck, shaking him. "Don't ya be daft, lad, or I'll beat the tar out o' ya."

Not this time, Willie thought. He thrust his right hand up through his father's arms and connected hard with his jaw. The man's head snapped back and he lost his grip. Willie turned and ran. He dashed through alleyways, down crowded streets and through vacant lots. He did not stop until he reached the woodpile behind Wakefield House where he collapsed panting.

Now what had he done? He couldn't believe he had hit his own father, not that he didn't deserve it. Willie sat with his back against the shed. Tears came to his eyes but he let them flow. He hadn't cried in years, but he did now. He cried for his long-dead mother, for the broken man his father had become, for Pete. He cried until he had no tears left. Then he wiped his face on his sleeve, stood up and began looking for a new hiding place for the pouch of coins that meant his freedom.

FRANK RUBBED HIS JAW. Half of him was mad as hell at his son. The other half was proud that the boy packed such a powerful punch. But it was the cash that Willie was carrying that was of real importance. The boy would be stashing it somewhere. He had run towards the beach. Maybe there. Not on the beach, surely, but by the sea wall. It was worth a look. Frank set off at a fast clip toward the ocean.

There were a few people, couples mostly, strolling on the wall. The farther north one went, Frank knew, the fewer people one would see. Soon he reached a deserted area. The wall was just a short step up on the landward side but four feet down to the sand on the ocean side. Willie had quite a head start, but it would take him time to find just the right spot, assuming he was here at all. Frank figured he might be able to catch him if he picked up his pace.

Soon he spied something on the ocean side. As he got closer he realized it was a person, a man, lying on the ground. Drawing closer yet he saw that the man was uncommonly still, face down and in an awkward position.

Frank jumped down off the wall and walked a bit hesitantly toward the prone form. "Hello?" he called. No response. He put his boot on the man's backside and gave a shove. No response to that either. The man never moved. Frank looked around. There was no one anywhere nearby. "Drunk are ya?" he asked.

A drunk man might well have money in his pocket, Frank thought, his son momentarily forgotten. He bent down and turned the man over then jerked back in alarm. He was staring at the sand-covered face of Samuel Thompson.

Frank's breath came in gulps. He closed and opened his fists. There was a lot of dried blood on Thompson's forehead – right where Frank had hit him the night before. "Sure it weren't me what killed ya," he said aloud. But his voice was shaky. There was no 'sure' about it.

Still, it was because of Thompson that Frank was short of cash. He'd only be taking his own money back, he reasoned. Huffing a bit, he knelt beside the body and made the sign of the cross – just in case. He knew that Thompson kept his folding money in his right vest pocket. Frank stuck his fingers in - nothing. He tried the other pocket – empty.

He was reaching into a pocket of Thompson's pants when he heard a scream. He jumped up to see two wide-eyed ladies standing on the sea wall above him. Both had their fingers to their lips. Frank turned and ran, faster than he ever had, until he could run no more. He collapsed to the ground panting hard and wondering who the hell those ladies were and what was going to happen next.

CHAPTER 10

*C*larissa and Emma clung to each other. "Oh dear Lord," Clarissa gasped, unable to take her eyes off the scene below her. Mr. Thompson looked like he was asleep or passed out.

Emma found her hands almost as shaky as her companion's, but she refused to give in to emotions that would render her useless. She urged Clarissa off the wall. "Stay here. I'm going to Mr. Thompson."

"No! You can't. You can't go over there."

"I have to. No matter what we think of him, he's unconscious and needs help." Taking a deep breath of the brisk sea air, Emma stepped back onto the wall, awkwardly sat down, then dropped down to the beach. Her courage began to fail her as she approached the body. His face was ashen but for a bruise that had darkened under one eye. "Mr. Thompson?"

"Oh Emma, do stop." Clarissa had turned and now looked down at Mr. Thompson's lifeless body. She started to tremble then swooned and slipped bonelessly to the ground.

"Clarissa!" Emma put her hands on the wall and tried to hoist herself back up, but it was too high. The incoming water had pushed sand higher at the wall a little farther north, so she ran to the dune and crossed over the wall, scraping her ankle and ripping the hem of her dress. Emma ran along beside the wall, nearly tripping as she rushed to the now-recovering Clarissa. Unmindful of the damage she was doing to her garments, Emma knelt before her.

"Are you alright?"

Clarissa sat up but closed her eyes. "Yes. I'll be fine."

"Ladies, whatever is going on here?"

Emma turned to see Dr. Grayson, accompanied by one of Captain Delgado's men, standing on the pathway.

"Oh, Doctor, I'm so glad to see you. Clarissa…."

"I'm fine," Clarissa interrupted. "I was only dizzy for a moment."

"Just sit here a minute. Miss Campbell, isn't it?"

Clarissa nodded.

"What brought this on?" Dr. Grayson asked, kneeling down and taking Clarissa's hand in his. "Do you often have dizzy spells?"

Clarissa shook her head but remained silent.

"Over there." Emma pointed across the wall. "It's Mr. Thompson."

The officer leaned forward. "Good God!" He hopped over the wall to kneel next to the body. "Doctor?"

Dr. Grayson joined him but it was obvious that Thompson was dead. Standing, the doctor shook his head then hoisted himself back over the wall. "I am so sorry you had to witness this," he said, glad to see that the color had returned to Clarissa's pale cheeks. He reached down for Emma's hands. "Here, let's get you both on your feet again."

"It's worse than you know." Clarissa found her voice as Emma and the doctor helped her up. "We saw the killer."

"You witnessed the murder?"

"We did not," Emma replied. "And we can't really say it was the killer we saw, although it is certainly possible."

The officer vaulted back over the wall. "If you don't mind my asking, what did you see?"

"A man was searching through Mr. Thompson's clothing." Emma shuddered at the memory as Clarissa started to sway again. Grabbing Clarissa's arm to steady her, the doctor turned to the officer.

"That will be enough for now. These ladies have had quite an experience. I'm going to escort Miss Campbell and Mrs.Wakefield home. They'll be more comfortable answering questions there."

The young officer hesitated only a moment before nodding in agreement.

"Ladies." Dr. Grayson kept his arm around Clarissa and offered his other arm to Emma.

She slipped her hand into the crook of Dr. Grayson's elbow, grateful for the strength she felt. A moment later she heard a shrill whistle as the officer summoned additional help.

Despite the warmth of the evening, Dr. Grayson asked Gibbs to light a fire in the parlor. Emma sat next to Clarissa on the sofa and found herself grateful for the shawl the doctor had placed about her shoulders. Since they'd arrived home she found she couldn't stop shivering.

"Drink this." The doctor offered them each a glass of whiskey.

Clarissa accepted the glass, downed it in one long gulp, then gasped as she nearly rose off the sofa choking and trying to catch her breath.

"You didn't need to drink it all at once." The doctor smiled gently. "But it will help to warm you."

Clarissa patted her chest. "It certainly does," she said breathlessly. "My goodness, you might have warned me." She looked at Emma who still clutched her glass with both hands. "Why aren't you drinking?" she challenged.

Emma looked up, her eyes dark and haunted. "I think I know who that man was," she said quietly.

"What?"

"The man who was kneeling over poor Mr. Thompson."

"Poor Mr. Thompson? Poor Mr. Thompson?" Clarissa's voice rose in agitation. "He's the bastard who killed my Andrew!"

Emma turned to Clarissa. "Oh, I'm so sorry. I didn't mean that. I meant…" her eyes filled with tears. "I'm sorry," she gulped. "It's just…"

"No, I'm sorry." Clarissa reached over and pried one of Emma's hands off the glass she still held. "You were the one kind enough to see if you could help the man even though we knew him to be a cad."

"You both have been through an ordeal," the doctor broke in, afraid that in another moment he would have two sobbing women on his hands. "Drink up, Mrs. Wakefield. Doctor's orders." Reaching over he gently urged the glass to Emma's lips making her take a sip. She shuddered once, but much to his relief seemed to find her composure again.

"Mrs. Wakefield?" Gibbs stood in the doorway. "An officer has arrived and has asked to speak with you. Shall I send him in?"

Unsure of her voice at the moment, Emma nodded.

The same officer who had accompanied the doctor earlier stepped hesitantly into the parlor. "Beg pardon, ladies, and I hate to add to your distress, but I do need to ask a few questions."

Emma took a deep breath and forced herself to remain calm. "Would you like a drink, sir? The good doctor will be happy to provide you with one." She lifted her own glass as proof.

"Thank you no, not at the moment." He pulled a straight chair over to sit next to the doctor across from the ladies. "Can you tell me what happened?"

"It's my fault." Clarissa's eyes were now overly bright and her cheeks flushed from the drink. "After we told Captain Delgado that we thought Mr. Thompson had killed my Andrew, I insisted we take a walk."

"But we decided not to walk into town," Emma added. "We didn't want to bump into Mr. Thompson." Her voice began to shake again.

"I wanted to walk along the sea wall," Clarissa continued. "I wanted to feel the fresh air on my face. Do we really need the fire going?" she questioned, giving the high neckline of her dress a tug. "It's gotten so warm in here."

The officer gave the doctor a look, who in turn gave a meaningful glance to the empty glass in Clarissa's hand. "I'm sure things will cool off shortly," he said turning back to Emma. "So you were walking on the sea wall?"

Emma nodded. "That's when we saw him."

"That's when you saw Mr. Thompson?"

"No, that other man," Clarissa interrupted. "The one in the raggedy clothes." She turned to Emma. "He looked like a bum, didn't he?"

"You saw a bum while you were walking?" the officer asked warily.

Emma took another deep breath. "We were walking when we noticed a man bending over another who was lying in the sand on the beach side of the wall."

"We screamed," Clarissa interrupted again, "when we saw him that is." She gave a small hiccup and pressed her fingers to her lips. "Oh, excuse me."

"We were startled," Emma continued. "One doesn't expect

to see something like that and to be honest, at first we weren't really sure what we were seeing. I thought the man in the sand had fallen and his friend was trying to help him up."

"But that wasn't the case…" the officer prompted.

Emma shook her head. "It looked like he was going through the man's pockets."

"Probably to rob him," Clarissa added with a nod.

"When he saw us, he turned and ran."

"That's ssswhat thieves do," Clarissa said as her words began to slur. "They run away. Or they tell you their wife is dead and then suddenly she appears." Clarissa made a poofing sound and clapped her hands together.

"I think it's time for Miss Campbell to be escorted home." Dr. Grayson stood.

"Just a few minutes more." The officer turned back to Emma. "Could you describe the man who ran away?"

"Yes, but I believe I know who he is." She took another deep breath. "From where we were standing it looked like Frank Jefferson."

The officer frowned. "How do you know Frank Jefferson?"

"I really don't." She looked down at the glass she still clutched in one hand. "Sadie, my cook, pointed him out to me at the market the other day. He was causing a… a commotion with the fishmonger and I asked Sadie who he was. She told me it was Frank Jefferson."

"I see. And do you know how Miss Sadie would know the likes of Frank Jefferson?"

Emma began to shiver again. "His son, Willie, often helps Sadie carry things from the market."

≈

RACHEL THOMPSON OPENED the door and stepped back as her brother stumbled into the room, nearly landing on top of her. "Well look what the cat dragged in." She waved a hand in front of her face. "Good grief, Scott, did you drink the place dry last night?" He turned and she saw the bruise that darkened one eye. "So besides getting drunk and smelling like a skunk, you were in a fight as well?"

"Went to find that cheating husband of yours." He glanced about her tiny room as if he were unsure where he was. "Planned to teach him a lesson. Gonna make him come back to you, but don't for the life of me know why you'd want the bastard." He flopped down on the bed with a groan.

"You got into a fight with Samuel?"

"Yep, got the bastard good and proper."

Rachel stared hard at her brother. "I told you I'd already taken care of that. Don't you ever listen to me?"

"Ha! Don't see him running back to you, do I?"

Rachel rolled her eyes. "Unlike you, I don't need to rely on violence. And he'll be running back to me. In fact, I'll wager he'll be here before the day is through."

"And just how do you plan on that?" Clearly fascinated, Scott sat up. "You gonna wave a magic wand and the bastard appears?"

"There's no magic about it. I simply sent him a box of candy."

Scott laughed out loud then grabbed his head. "Thompson's going to race back to you because of candy?"

She nodded as a grin tugged at her lips. "I bought a box of his favorite confections and simply added a new ingredient. A little rat poison for my rat of a husband."

"What? I thought you wanted him back, not dead."

"Oh, he won't die." She picked up a brush to stroke the curls that hung over her shoulder. "I know my husband well. He'll eat one piece and his stomach will start to protest.

Samuel can't abide feeling poorly. You might even say that he's afraid of illness. It terrifies him more than anything." Her smile grew. "I'll wager he'll be here before the noonday meal begging me to create a cure for him."

Scott's brow drew together. "You sound like you've done this before."

"Of course I have. How do you think I've kept him in line these past years?"

"You've been feeding him poison for years?"

Rachel shrugged. "Only when necessary or I needed to teach him a lesson, like now. It's perfectly safe," she continued, setting down her brush. "He'd have to eat more than half the box to do any real damage and he'd never do that. No, right now I don't have to do anything but wait for him to show up and beg for my forgiveness. But in the meantime, you need to make yourself scarce."

EMMA WOKE WITH A START, pulling herself from the nightmare of her dreams. Lighting the candle on her bedside table, she sat back on the edge of the bed and hugged herself against the early morning chill. That damned column, she thought, replaying the words from the *Cat's Meow* in her mind. The newspaper column was often witty and full of fun, but the one she had read just before retiring had turned dark with words of gloom.

All night her mind had circled round and round with the events from the day before, mixing with the column's forecast of disaster, jerking her awake each time she closed her eyes. She still couldn't believe that she'd harbored a killer and never suspected. True, she had deduced he wasn't the textile salesman he had claimed to be, but dear Lord in heaven, she'd almost convinced herself he was an agent with the

Secret Service. Now the realization that he'd had a hand in Andrew's death was making her head spin. And where was Howard? Had he played a part in Mr. Thompson's death?

The clock told her that the hour was very early, but she knew it was useless to try to rest any longer. Rising, she quickly dressed for the day then perched again on the edge of her bed. Her head ached and despite splashing cold water on her face, her eyes felt heavy from lack of sleep. Somehow she was going to have to erase the image of Frank Jefferson kneeling over Mr. Thompson's dead body if she was going to get through the day.

Reaching for her shawl she pulled it around her shoulders. What would happen when the police found Frank Jefferson? Surely they'd take the man to jail. Would there be a trial? And dear Lord would she have to give testimony as to what she and Clarissa had seen? She hugged herself tighter and wondered if Clarissa had managed to find sleep any better than she had. Deciding not to tarry any longer, she blew out the candle and let the last light of the moon guide her way.

From the balcony she could see that lanterns already glowed in the kitchen and she quickly made her way downstairs and across the yard, eager for company to take her mind in a different direction.

Sadie looked up as Emma entered. "You shouldn't be up so early after the day you had yesterday."

"I couldn't sleep," Emma perched on a stool at the work table.

"You could have asked the doctor for some laudanum. That would do the trick."

Emma shuddered. "No thank you. But I'd love a strong cup of tea when the kettle's ready."

Tobias stepped into the kitchen with an armload of wood

and stopped when he saw Emma. "Everything all right, Mrs. Wakefield?"

"Of course it's not all right," Sadie snapped. "The missus saw a man killed yesterday. How could anything be all right?"

Tobias cringed and turned to Emma. "I didn't mean…"

Emma just shook her head which only intensified the growing ache. "Don't worry, Tobias. We'll get through this. I just wish I didn't see the image every time I close my eyes."

Sadie placed a steaming mug of tea on the table and gave Emma a long stare. "You want some whiskey to go in that?"

Emma felt her stomach roil at the thought. "Ah, no thank you. But if there's a leftover piece of bread I'd like that."

Sadie set the bread basket in front of Emma and went back to her batter. "I'm doing corn cakes to go with the rashers of salty bacon," she said as she continued to stir. "The porridge will be done shortly and there's cold tongue and a kidney pie."

"It sounds delicious," Emma said even as her stomach threatened to revolt.

"I hope when the Captain comes down to break his fast he can tell us that Frank Jefferson be in jail and locked up tight," Tobias said as he shoved wood into the baking oven. "That man be a drunk and a menace if you ask me."

"Don't remember anyone asking you," Sadie snapped, then softening her tone she shook her head. "Sit down and start your breakfast." She set his coffee mug on the table across from Emma. "But don't go distressing Mrs. Wakefield with talk of the likes of Frank Jefferson." She gave her husband a gentle cuff on the shoulder.

Emma stirred her tea then took a tentative sip. "I've been wondering," she said finally, "if they put Frank Jefferson in jail for killing Mr. Thompson, what will happen to Willie?"

Sadie turned around her eyes filled with concern. "I never

thought that far," she said slowly. "I was just happy the mister would be in jail."

"Don't know as it would make much difference," Tobias said, as he bit into a slice of bacon. "Jefferson don't do anything for the boy as it is."

"Well he can't stay by himself." Emma frowned. "And he's really not old enough to get an apprenticeship."

Gibbs stepped into the kitchen. "Am I tardy this morning?" he asked horrified, as he hastily reached for his pocket watch to check the time.

Emma gave a tired smile. "We're just getting an early start," glad that the half piece of dried bread and tea had somewhat calmed her stomach. Now if she could just ease the ache in her head, she'd be ready to face the day.

LATER THAT MORNING, Emma sat at her desk and made a list of what needed her attention. Andrew's possessions would have to be boxed and sent to his parents. Then she could ready the room for a new guest. The very thought brought tears to her eyes. Andrew had been one of her first tenants. How she would miss his clever wit and cheerful demeanor. She decided to send a note to Clarissa to see if she wanted to help with Andrew's things.

Then there was Mr. Thompson's room to deal with. She would need to box his possessions also. Should she send word to Mrs. Thompson to come and collect them? Emma frowned. The thought of dealing with Rachel Thompson again was far from pleasant as she remembered the missing silver spoon. Perhaps it would be more prudent to simply take the items to her.

Emma turned at the knock at her door. "Yes?" But her eyes grew wide when it was Dr. Grayson who entered.

"I brought you something for your headache."

Emma blinked. "But how did…"

Grayson smiled and his dimple flashed. "My dear Mrs. Wakefield, I'm a doctor. One only had to look at you this morning to see the pain that is pounding behind your eyes."

She eyed the small vial he carried. "I'm not taking any laudanum."

"That's good to know because I wouldn't prescribe it." He moved to stand behind her chair. "Now I just want you to sit here and relax for a moment."

She stiffened as she felt his fingertips rest on either side of her forehead.

"I promise not to hurt you. Just relax. I have some rose oil and I think that might do the trick."

The scent of the oil was pleasant and reminded her of the roses that bloomed in her garden each spring. The pressure of his fingers on her temples increased but not unpleasantly, and Emma felt herself begin to relax. At some point one hand moved to the back of her neck and his strong fingers made quick work of the tension there. She felt herself going limp and struggled not to slump over in her chair.

"There," he said finally, giving the back of her neck one last stroke which now felt more like a caress. "I want you to just sit here for awhile with your eyes closed and relax. Let the oil do its work."

She felt a brush on the top of her head and then she heard him move away and cross the room. The door closed with a quiet click and Emma knew she was once again alone. For several moments she didn't move. The scent of the rose oil was so pleasant, and she felt so relaxed that she hated to open her eyes. It took another moment for her to realize her headache was indeed gone. Gingerly she reached up to touch her temples. The ache that had plagued her all night had finally vanished. Then her hand lifted to her hair. Had the doctor kissed her on the top of her head, the way one might kiss away the hurt on a child? She shivered with the thought. Don't be absurd, she chided, giving herself a shake. You're a woman not a child and he's a doctor. It shouldn't concern you that his eyes twinkle each time he smiles. Pulling herself back to the work at hand, Emma rose with new determination. She'd send the note to Clarissa then she'd deal with Mrs. Thompson.

CHAPTER 11

*W*aiting for a response from her note to Clarissa, Emma stepped into the kitchen to find Sadie muttering to herself and angrily pulling turnips from her basket. "What's wrong?"

Sadie paused and looked up. "I don't know what some folks can be thinking these days."

Emma looked round but could not find the cause of the woman's distress. "Did Henny disappear again?"

Sadie shook her head then all but slammed the basket down on the floor. "At the market," she said taking a breath, "I heard that Frank Jefferson was arrested. He's in jail even as we speak."

"But that's good news, isn't it?" Clearly confused, Emma frowned and perched on a stool.

"If that was the end of it." Sadie stormed over to the pump and filled the kettle.

"Then what else has happened?"

"I'll tell you." Sadie checked the wood in the stove then plopped the kettle on the top. "They've also arrested Willie."

"What? Arrested Willie! Whatever for?"

Sadie wiped her hands then sat on her own stool as anger drained her energy. "I don't know, but the word is that Frank Jefferson was the one to point a finger at him."

"His own father accused him? But who would believe a thing like that?"

"Someone must because I heard more than once that the detectives came and took the boy away early this morning."

"That can't be right." Emma rose and started to pace.

"You might ask the Captain when he comes for the noonday meal," Sadie suggested. "He'll tell you straight."

Emma stopped. "I'm not waiting until then. I'm marching down to the jail right this minute and demanding they let that poor boy out." She tugged off her apron and tossed it on the table. "If I'm late getting back…"

"You see to getting that boy out of jail and Gibbs and I will tend to the meal," Sadie said, nodding in approval. "You bring him back here so we can at least feed the poor soul. No telling when his last meal was."

"I'll do that. But first I'm going to give a good piece of my mind to whoever is in charge." And with that she stormed past Gibbs as he entered the kitchen.

Gibbs looked from Sadie to Emma's retreating form. "What has happened to put the missus in such a state?" As Sadie explained, Gibbs felt his own anger grow. "And they locked the boy up?"

Sadie nodded. "Got it directly from Mrs. Brown who lives but two houses down from the Jeffersons. She said she watched them detective fellows come and take the boy away around daybreak."

"And Mrs. Wakefield is headed to the jail?"

Sadie nodded again.

"I wouldn't want to be the one at the receiving end of her anger." Gibbs started to grin.

"Ain't that the truth." Sadie picked up a turnip and struggled not to smile as she started to peel it. "Ain't that the truth."

~

EMMA STOOD in front of the bars of the holding cell, arms akimbo. "You will tell me right this minute how you came by so much money, Willie Jefferson." She realized she sounded a bit breathless, as she had walked at a good clip down to King Street.

Willie stood in the back corner of the cell, shifting his weight from foot to foot. He had been on the floor there, his head buried between his drawn up knees, but had sprung to his feet when he saw her.

Her heart went out to him. She was quite sure that Willie had not stolen the pouch of coins that the officer at the front desk had told her about, but he would have to admit where he had come by the money or he'd be following his father across the road to the main prison.

"I'm sorry, Mrs. Wakefield. I can't. But I didn't steal it; honest, ma'am. I ain't never stole nothin'."

"Willie, if you are going to get out of here, you are going to have to tell us how you got that money. You don't want to stay here, do you?"

Willie hung his head. "No, ma'am, but I promised."

"Promised? Who did you promise?"

He looked at her squarely. "I can't say, ma'am."

Emma sighed. She could see his determination in the set of his jaw. "Are they feeding you?"

Willie nodded.

The cell was small, but it was cleaner than Emma had expected it to be, and Willie was alone – at least for the moment. He was safe but for how long?

"Willie, promise me that when you come to your senses

you'll ask for me. Promise?"

"Yes, ma'am."

EMMA WALKED SWIFTLY BACK to Wakefield House. How was she going to convince Willie to tell where he'd found the money? Gibbs met her at the gate when she returned.

"Madam?"

"He won't say where he got all that money. Says he made a promise not to."

Gibbs nodded. "If I may suggest, Mrs. Wakefield, the boy made a friend in Tobias. Perhaps he could help."

"Thank you. It's certainly worth a try."

Emma sat in the kitchen with a cup of tea as she waited for Tobias to return with more firewood.

"I don't know what's taking that man so long," Sadie wiped her hands on a cloth. "Let me fetch him for you." Just as Sadie opened the door Tobias stumbled through, his arms laden with firewood.

He dropped the wood by the stove, took out a rag to wipe the sweat off his face, and turning to the table, gave a little bow. "Mrs. Wakefield."

"Tobias, I was just telling Sadie that they are holding Willie because he had quite a bit of money on his person when they picked him up and he won't say where he got it. The authorities believe he might have had something to do with Mr. Thompson's death. Evidently Mr. Thompson had money at McConnell's but when he was found, his pockets were empty."

"Willie wouldn't take money from a dead man!"

"I agree." Sadie folded her arms over her chest. "He's a good boy."

"I agree with both of you. But where could he have gotten so much money?"

Tobias cleared his throat. "I'm sure he earned it honest-like."

"Not from the few coins he makes as a delivery boy. Tobias, Willie likes you. Perhaps you could get him to tell his secret. Would you go down to the jail and have a word with him? Please?"

Tobias backed up a little. He looked at Emma, then Sadie, then back again to Emma. Tears began to form in his eyes. "I'm so sorry, Mrs. Wakefield. I don't has to ask him. I know where he got some of them coins."

"What?" The two women spoke in unison.

He took a deep breath. "It's me that gave them to him."

"What…" Emma couldn't believe what she was hearing.

"I didn't want to lose my job," Tobias hurried on but kept his eyes downcast.

Sadie walked over to face him. "Explain yourself," she ordered.

He took a ragged breath. "For a time, it's Willie thats been doin' some of my chores and I been paying him for it."

"For how long a time?" Sadie asked.

"He be choppin' most the wood since last winter." Tobias looked at Emma. "He's real good at it, ma'am. And my old back … well it just ain't what is used to be."

"And why didn't you tell me, you silly old man?" Sadie chided.

"On account of my job. I didn't want ya to know I couldn't do some stuff no more. And I didn't see as it were hurtin' anybody. Like I said, we was real careful."

Emma rose. "I'm going back to the jail and get that boy out. We'll deal with the rest of this when I return."

"Will they just give him to you?" Sadie asked, looking decidedly uncomfortable. "I mean, no disrespect ma'am, but…"

Emma put up her hand. "You're right." She thought a

moment. "I'll speak with Captain Delgado first." Checking the time, Emma realized that the Captain would most likely be walking back to Wakefield House for his noonday meal. She decided that if she walked to the jail again she would likely meet him along the way. She fetched a few essentials from her office, advised Gibbs of her plan, and made her way down Charlotte Street.

She had gone about halfway when she saw the Captain.

He nodded, "Morning, Mrs. Wakefield."

"Good morning, Captain."

"I understand you were talking to young Willie this morning."

"I was. And now I know where the money came from." Emma explained about Tobias' and Willie's partnership. "And he had promised Tobias that he would tell no one of their dealings," she finished.

Captain Delgado let out a low whistle. "So he'd rather go to jail than betray a friend." He frowned at her. "And you are on your way to...?"

"Get him out."

He raised an eyebrow. "His father is still incarcerated, you know."

"I do. But I have the means to keep an eye on him. I'll take full responsibility."

The captain nodded. "I thought you might. I'll accompany you back."

"No need, Captain. I don't want you to miss your dinner." She produced a small notebook and pencil from her bag. "If you would write a note to your officers, I'm sure they would release Willie to me on your recommendation."

The Captain laughed. "I see you have come fully prepared." He took the notebook and wrote a few lines then signed his name with a flourish.

THE OFFICER at the desk read the note and smiled. "I'm happy to let this one go," he said. He opened a locked desk drawer and retrieved a large coin pouch and a small pocket knife. "These are his." He handed the items to Emma. "You know Captain Delgado wants you to hold the money till everything is settled."

Emma nodded.

The officer went down the short hallway, returned a moment later with Willie whom he had grabbed by the scruff of the neck.

Emma was taken aback until she saw the conspiratorial grin the officer was wearing. "Now don't you be getting into any trouble, Willie Jefferson," he said sternly, leaning over so his nose was an inch from Willie's. "You be a proper gentleman with Mrs. Wakefield. You hear?" He gave the boy a light cuff on the head and pushed him toward Emma.

Willie uttered a weak "Yes, sir."

By the time Emma returned to Wakefield House with Willie in tow the noonday meal was nearly over. "You go back to the kitchen," she told the boy, "and don't get in the way. I'll be along shortly."

"Yes, ma'am." Willie took off at a trot.

"I presume everyone has been fed," she said to Gibbs as she entered the house.

"Yes ma'am, and the meal was declared most delicious as always."

Emma sighed with relief. In the dining room Henny and Sadie were clearing the tables as the last of the house guests went their separate ways. Sadie looked up at Emma, an unspoken question in her expression.

"We have him. I sent him to the kitchen. I'll meet you there in a few minutes."

Emma picked up a stack of dishes to be washed as she passed a table and noted she was carrying twice the number of plates as Henny. This wasn't going to continue, she decided. But first she was going to deal with Willie and Tobias.

She found Willie and Tobias sitting on a wooden bench just outside the kitchen door, both looking worried. "Willie, go inside and ask Sadie to put the kettle on for tea. We'll be in shortly." She turned to Tobias. "Tobias, there will always be a place for you here at Wakefield House. Always. But this arrangement with Willie has to end."

"But missus…"

Emma held up a hand to stop his words. "I will hire Willie to chop the wood from now on. You will be responsible for overseeing his work. Now, are there any other chores that are causing you pain?"

Tobias looked down at the ground and shook his head.

"Then we'll consider this matter closed. But as time goes on if you feel there is another chore you can't complete you'll pass that on to Willie also. Do you understand?"

When Tobias looked up again his eyes were wet with tears.

"Good, now I never again want you to entertain the notion that you would be fired. This is your home, Tobias, and always will be." She turned to Sadie who was standing in the doorway. "I'm going to tell Henny to put up a pallet in the laundry room for Willie. He can sleep there."

Sadie looked from Tobias then back to Emma. "Ah…"

"You have another idea?"

"If you wouldn't mind, Mrs. Wakefield, we have space."

It had been quite a while since Emma had been in the little house behind the wood shed where the couple lived. "Are you sure?"

They both nodded enthusiastically and the matter was settled.

Later when she still hadn't heard from Clarissa, Emma

decided to go and check on her before she dealt with anything else. Knowing how upset she herself had been after seeing Thompson's dead body, she could only imagine how Clarissa must be feeling. First losing Andrew in such a horrific way, finding Thompson was his killer, then finding Thompson dead. Emma shuddered and forced herself to concentrate on something other than the images that seemed to haunt her every moment.

Deciding another walk would do her some good, she set out for the Campbell's. The changeable weather was warm but not uncomfortable as she made her way down King Street. As she walked she thought of young Willie. At least she'd been successful in getting him released from jail. She still couldn't fathom a father that would so gladly accuse his only child of such a deed in order to try to save his own skin. But now that she had Willie at Wakefield House she needed to decide how best to help him.

When she finally reached the Campbell's, Watson showed her to the family's front parlor while he went to see if Miss Clarissa was receiving. It didn't take long but when the door opened it wasn't Clarissa but her brother Jonathan who entered.

"Mrs. Wakefield." He stepped farther into the room then made his way to the trolley that contained the family's liquor supply. "May I offer you some refreshment?"

"No, thank you." Emma had perched on the edge of the sofa and as Jonathan drew closer, his bruised split-lip was very apparent.

"I'm glad to have the chance to speak with you," he said, pouring himself a generous drink then sinking into a chair. "I know my sister has been trying to put on a brave front about losing Andrew. But I need you to know it's all an act."

"An act?"

"She wouldn't want me to tell you this, but she spends

most of her time in her room crying. I truly think her heart is broken." Jonathan rubbed the whiskey glass across his forehead with a weary gesture. "And it breaks my heart to see her this way. I don't know how she's going to survive this."

Thinking of her own dear James, Emma looked down at her clenched hands. "It's never easy getting past losing a loved one," she said quietly. "And you're right, I'm sure her heart does feel broken."

"I only hope Thompson's death can give her some closure." Jonathan took a sip of his whiskey. "If I had known what a despicable bastard he was, I would have seen to things sooner. How's Howard making out?"

"Howard?"

"Surely you knew he was at McConnell's that night. Got in some good ones before the lights went out."

"The lights went out?" Emma struggled to make sense of what she was hearing. Had Jonathan just admitted he and Howard had had something to do with Thompson's demise?

Jonathan grinned, then winced as the motion pulled at his lip. "Let's just say we decided to teach the bastard a lesson he'd never forget. And now he never will."

With that statement hanging in the air, Jonathan pulled himself out of his chair as the parlor door opened and Clarissa came in.

"Emma, I'm so sorry to have kept you waiting." Clarissa crossed the room to take Emma's hands. "I trust my brother kept you company in the interim?"

"Ladies," Jonathan raised his glass, gave a nod then left the room.

"Oh I do wish he wouldn't drink so much," Clarissa said watching him leave. "But I fear this business with Thompson has affected him more than I would have thought."

Still reeling from the possibility that Howard and Jonathan had somehow been involved in Thompson's death,

Emma could only stare at the closed door. Was it possible they were to blame and not Frank Jefferson? And if they were, how would Clarissa deal with the fact her beloved brother was charged with murder? And Emma wondered how she could go on if she lost another cousin.

"I took something to help me sleep last night," Clarissa was saying when Emma pulled herself back to the present. "And I fear it's made me slower than molasses this morning. I did get a good night's sleep, but I don't think I'll be doing that again." She frowned. "I don't like waking up and feeling like I have a head full of cotton wool. But I say, Emma, are you quite all right? You look so pale."

Emma straightened and forced a smile. "I'm fine." She took a breath. "You mentioned before that you had wanted to see the woman that claimed to be Mr. Thompson's wife. I'm going over to Spruce House where she's staying to ask what she wants done with her husband's possessions. I wondered if you would wish to accompany me?"

"Absolutely. I know I should feel some sympathy for the woman, after all she just lost her husband. But I fear I can't." Clarissa stood. "Let me have Watson fetch us a carriage then we can go."

"It's not that far. I thought we might walk."

Clarissa shook her head. "No, we are going to arrive in style. It's not that I'd mind the walk, but for this appointment we are not going to arrive covered in street dust."

"Oh my." Emma looked down and realized her own gown now wore a fine layer of dust from the road.

Clarissa reached for a bell pull that hung by the wall mirror. "I'll call my maid and she'll have you spotless before Watson can announce the carriage is ready."

True to her word, Emma's dress was brushed and they were ready even as Watson called them for the carriage.

In the carriage Clarissa gave Emma a quizzical stare. "What are you going to say to the woman?"

Emma blinked. "I really hadn't thought that far ahead." She paused. "I guess I'm simply going to offer my condolences and ask what her wishes are for her husband's possessions."

"You'll let her come to Wakefield House to collect them?"

At this Emma shook her head. "No, I will offer to pack them and have them delivered to her."

"Then would I be too forward to ask if I may help you with that chore?" Clarissa's expression turned fierce. "I wouldn't want any more of Andrew's things to be mistakenly handed over."

"Of course you must assist me." Emma reached for Clarissa's hand and gave a squeeze. "I was going to ask if you felt up to going through them with me."

"I'd like nothing better," Clarissa declared. "Just the thought of that man touching Andrew's possessions makes my stomach turn."

The carriage made short work of the trip and as the driver helped them down, Emma recognized Rachel Thompson coming from the boarding house's dining room.

"Mrs. Thompson," she called, making the woman turn and glance in their direction. "May we speak with you a moment?"

"Concerning what?"

"Perhaps there is some place where we might speak in private?"

Rachel stared at them for a long moment. "I recognize Mrs. Wakefield, but who might you be?"

"I'm Clarissa Campbell," Clarissa said sweetly, even as she managed to look down her nose at Thompson's wife in a manner that Emma knew only the most elite of society could manage.

"We really need to speak with you," Emma added quickly. "Is there a parlor we might make use of?"

"Follow me." Rachel turned and moved down the walkway to a door at the end. She opened the door, glanced inside, and finding the room empty, motioned for them to follow.

Once inside Emma couldn't help herself as she appraised the parlor's furnishings. The upholstery was showing definite signs of wear and all the furniture was in want of a good polish.

"What's this all about?" Rachel turned to face them.

"I wanted to offer my sympathies," Clarissa said, when Emma remained silent.

"Sympathies for what?" Rachel snapped, clearly irritated by the encounter.

Clarissa exchanged an uncertain glance with Emma. Was it possible the woman didn't know?

"For the loss of your husband," Emma said quietly.

"What are you talking about?"

"I'm sorry. I thought the authorities would have contacted you by now."

"Samuel's dead?" Rachel's voice shook and she sank slowly onto the closest chair.

"Should I call someone for you?" Emma prompted, alarmed at how pale the woman had become.

"Just tell me what happened. And how is it that you found out?" she demanded. "No one has bothered to contact me."

"We had the unfortunate experience of finding the body," Clarissa declared. "He was lying on the ocean side of the sea wall."

"Had he fallen? I'm not familiar with this town. Did he fall from some great height?"

Emma shook her head. "The seawall isn't that high. It appeared that Mr. Thompson was struck on the head." She tried to push Jonathan's words, 'we decided to teach the bastard a lesson,' from her mind.

"And you were sent to tell me?"

"No," Emma said slowly. "We thought you would have already heard. Since he was boarding at Wakefield House, I came to ask what you wanted done with your husband's possessions."

"I'll come to collect them immediately," Rachel surged to her feet.

"Ah that won't be necessary," Emma said firmly. "I'll have everything collected and sent here so you won't need to make the trip."

"I'd rather come now," Rachel stated, as if that settled it.

"Well, I'm afraid that's not convenient," Emma said smoothly. "But I will see that you receive the items in a timely fashion. Tell me, how long are you planning to stay in our city?"

"I don't think I'm comfortable with some servant going through my Samuel's possessions," Rachel said. "Who knows what might disappear in the process."

Clarissa gasped at the insult but Emma only offered a tight smile. "You needn't worry about that. I'll personally see to the packing." Emma turned and nodding toward Clarissa started toward the door. "Your husband's items will be delivered to you before the day is through." And with that final declaration the two left the boarding house and climbed back into Clarissa's carriage.

CHAPTER 12

When the carriage returned to Wakefield House, Gibbs opened the door and assisted Emma and Clarissa down. "A word, Mrs. Wakefield, if I may."

Emma nodded. "Clarissa, why don't you wait for me in the parlor. I'll be along momentarily." She waited until Clarissa stepped away before turning back to Gibbs. "Has Mr. Langley returned yet?"

Gibbs shook his head. "Did you move the last bottle of pear wine?" he asked quietly, as he watched Clarissa make her way down the veranda.

"No, there's still one bottle in the dining room."

Gibbs shook his head again. "It's missing. I went to retrieve it from the cupboard to serve at supper this evening but the bottle was gone. I thought you might have moved it."

"No, I know it was there the day before yesterday because I saw it after breakfast when I was straightening up. Did you ask Daisy?"

"Pear wine isn't her favorite," Gibbs said with a small smile, "as she reminded me in no uncertain terms."

"Well, she's right about that. She never really approved

when James made the stuff or then when you continued after he died. It takes a good glass of whiskey to make *her* happy."

"Do you think one of the guests…."

"I don't know what's going on," Emma sighed wearily. "I know Mr. Thompson took Aunt Daisy's cameo because I found it in his room. But the money missing from my office was such a small amount it doesn't make sense that he would have been the one to take it." She rubbed at the ache that had started again behind her eyes. "Perhaps he took the wine as a gift when he went to the Campbell's for dinner." Emma sighed. "I'll ask Clarissa."

Gibbs nodded. "Do you wish some refreshments?"

"Thank you, yes, a pot of very, very strong tea would be lovely."

EMMA ENTERED the downstairs parlor to find Clarissa and Dr. Grayson sitting on the sofa deep in conversation. The doctor rose as Emma stepped into the room. "Please sit," Emma lowered herself onto the rocking chair closest to them. "Clarissa, I have a strange question. Did Mr. Thompson ever bring a bottle of wine when he came to dine with you and the family?"

Clarissa blinked with surprise. "No, never. Why would you ask that?"

Emma shook her head. "Never mind."

"Miss Campbell was just telling me of your trip to see Mrs. Thompson," Dr. Grayson said. "I'm so sorry that task fell to you ladies."

"I thought knowing that Mr. Thompson had something to do with Andrew's death, I was going to get great pleasure telling his wife that someone had bashed him over the head and now *he* was dead." Clarissa looked down at her folded hands. "But it wasn't enjoyable at all. It was just very sad."

Emma caught Dr. Grayson's look of surprise before he reached over and patted Clarissa's hands.

"Telling someone of death is never easy."

Gibbs tapped lightly on the door, then entered with the tea cart.

"Why don't I pour." the doctor sat forward. "Mrs. Wakefield?"

"Please." Emma knew she was shirking her duties as hostess, but suddenly she felt exhausted.

He handed her a steaming cup of tea then looked at Clarissa.

"I don't think so," Clarissa said slowly. "Emma, I know I was going to help you sort though Mr. Thompson's belongings, but would you mind terribly if I rely on you to check for Andrew's things? Right now I really think I just want to go home to my bed."

Emma set down her tea cup and rose as Clarissa did. "Of course. I can manage. I appreciated your going with me today to see his wife. But now you should go home and get some rest. The past few days have been more than a little taxing."

Dr. Grayson rose as well. "Let me see you to your carriage, Miss Campbell. And please don't worry. I'll be happy to assist Mrs. Wakefield with her task." He offered Clarissa his arm and led her from the room.

Emma sat back down and gratefully picked up her tea. She'd see to Thompson's belongings, but first she was going to enjoy a few moments of quiet along with her tea.

When the doctor returned, he found her slowly rocking back and forth in the chair with her eyes closed. "Mrs. Wakefield?" he asked quietly.

"I'm not asleep," Emma said, opening her eyes. "I was just taking a moment."

The doctor sat on the edge of the sofa and leaned

forward. "I meant what I said before. I'm more than willing to assist you in packing Thompson's possessions. But are you up to a question first?"

Emma stopped rocking. "Of course."

"Then tell me, is it true that the authorities believe Thompson's death was the result of a blow to the head?"

Emma nodded then frowned. "You were there," she said slowly. "Surely you saw all the dried blood on his temple."

"I did, but the blow didn't appear to be that severe. I believe Mr. Thompson was poisoned."

"Poisoned! Are you sure?"

"I can't be positive until I visit the coroner and look more closely at the body. But a British chemist has devised a test that can detect the presence of arsenic. It's called the Marsh test but the coroner wouldn't necessarily run that if the authorities told him Thompson was in a brawl that night."

"Poison, but how? Who could have done that?"

"As for who, I believe there are several we could name that would want to see the man's end. And as for how, they only needed to put the poison into something he ate or drank."

Emma immediately thought of the missing wine bottle. "Could someone have put the poison in his wine?"

"That is certainly a possibility. But if he drank the poison when he was at McConnell's that night, then more than likely he would have died there."

"But he died at the sea wall blocks away..." Emma pictured Thompson lying in the sand and Frank Jefferson leaning over him. Had Willie's father had a bottle with him? She couldn't remember seeing one but... "I need to go back to the sea wall," she stood suddenly.

"Have you thought of something?"

"Gibbs told me we are missing bottle of wine. Now it's

certainly possible that one of the guests has simply helped himself and forgotten to mention it or plans to tell me at supper tonight. But if Mr. Thompson was the one to take it…." Emma flopped back down on the rocker. "Never mind. I don't know what I was thinking. Mr. Thompson wouldn't poison himself." She gave a shudder. "No, I need to see to Mr. Thompson's possessions. I promised his wife I'd have them delivered today."

"Then let me assist you," the doctor said as they both stood.

With the doctor's help it didn't take long to pack Thompson's clothing back into his large valise. When they arrived at Spruce House, Emma was surprised to find Mrs. Thompson standing on the veranda speaking with an older woman. The doctor helped Emma from the carriage then reached back inside to withdraw the valise.

"Mrs. Thompson," Emma called, "may I have a word?"

Rachel Thompson dismissed the older woman then walked slowly toward Emma. "I assume you brought my husband's possessions?"

"Yes." Emma hesitated as Dr. Grayson set the valise at Mrs. Thompson's feet. "But I fear I also have more news to share with you." When Rachel said nothing but bent down to open the case, Emma went on. "I fear when I was here earlier I gave you some misinformation. I believe Miss Campbell said that Mr. Thompson had been killed by a blow to the head. We now believe he didn't die that way. He was poisoned."

Rachel jerked to her feet. "What? Poisoned? Who told you that?"

"I did." Dr. Grayson stepped forward, alarmed at how the color had drained from Rachel's face. "Allow me to introduce myself. I'm Doctor Alex Grayson. I also reside at Wakefield House, as did your husband. I saw his body at the sea wall and I will testify that it was poison and not a blow to his head that killed him."

Rachel immediately dropped to her knees making the doctor quickly step forward again. But she brushed him away as she started pulling items of clothing from the valise. "Where is it?she snapped.

"What are you looking for?" Emma was now also concerned at the woman's lack of color.

Rachel stood and swayed until the doctor firmly took her arm. "I'm fine." She jerked free. "Francie!" Her voice was shrill and strong in the small courtyard.

Emma watched as a young girl, probably no more than eight years of age, hobbled down the steps. She was rail thin and, if possible, her mismatched clothing was even more threadbare than Willie's.

"Francie," Rachel struggled to calm herself as the girl stepped closer "didn't you take the package I gave you to Wakefield House for my husband?"

Francie blinked in surprise then glanced nervously from one adult to the other. She recognized Mrs. Wakefield but had no idea who the handsome gentleman was who stood beside her. "I did, missus." She looked up at Rachel. "But I thought it was for your brother."

Rachel turned back to Emma. "Are you sure these are all my husband's possessions?"

"Is something missing?" Emma asked, wondering if the woman was referring to the pouch of stolen jewelry she'd found under the mattress. Had his wife already known of Andrew's death and that her husband was a thief?

"I sent Mr. Thompson a box of his favorite chocolates, and it isn't here. Did you take it?"

The doctor stiffened at the accusation hurled at Emma. "That was uncalled for, Mrs. Thompson," he chided. "I assisted Mrs. Wakefield in packing your husband's things and his room was well checked before we left to come here. I can assure you there was no box of chocolates to be packed."

"He did receive them," Emma said quickly as she watched Rachel Thompson turn her anger toward the thin girl. "Francie, is it?" Emma looked at the child and received the barest nod. "Francie was a good messenger and I can state with a certainty they were delivered. I saw them on your husband's dresser myself. I can only assume that Mr. Thompson found your gift and consumed it."

"I see." Rachel turned back toward the doctor. "And you're positive he was poisoned?"

Dr. Grayson nodded. "I can assure you the authorities will do everything in their power to find who caused your husband's death."

Rachel straightened then looked at Francie. "Go back upstairs and wait for me there." The girl hobbled off and Rachel glanced back to Emma. "Thank you for bringing my husband's things but there is no reason for you to linger. Good day." And with that she turned and started toward the stairs at the end of the veranda, leaving the opened valise laying on the ground.

The doctor bent down and hastily shoved the discarded clothing back in the case then firmly closed the latch.

Emma blinked and looked up at him when he stood. "I think we were just dismissed."

Dr. Grayson frowned as he watched Rachel retreat. "If she was truly married to Mr. Thompson then I do believe they deserved each other. What a disagreeable woman."

"Well, she just lost her husband and in a horrific way," Emma said quietly.

Grayson looked down at her. "As usual you're too kind." Taking her arm he walked Emma to their waiting carriage. "Let me get you back home. This has been quite an ordeal for you as well."

"I'm fine, but what I'd really like to do is visit the sea wall. I can't get the image of Frank Jefferson leaning over Mr. Thompson out of my head. Perhaps if I view the scene again I can erase that image."

"Are you certain?"

Emma nodded.

RACHEL PACED from one end of her tiny room and back. Had she miscalculated the amount of poison she'd used in the candy? Or had her fool of a husband eaten more than one piece? Hastily she tossed her clothing into the two bags she had carried with her. One thing was certain, she couldn't wait around for the authorities to start their inquiry. Francie would be able to tell them that the package had come from her. Rachel paused in her packing to consider. Somehow she had to get rid of Francie so the girl couldn't point a finger at her. Shoving her bags under the bed, she stepped to the doorway and called for the girl.

"Yes, missus?"

"Francie, be a dear and run to the stables and fetch a carriage for me."

"Are you going away?"

"No, just taking a short trip for the afternoon. I'll be back before supper. Here." She pulled several coins from her pocket. "These are for you. You're such a help to me."

Francie beamed down at the treasure in her hand. "I'll be quick as I can, missus." And turning, she hurried from the room.

Rachel pulled her bags from under the bed and finished packing. Then a few hasty words with the hotel's owner and her plan was set.

"The carriage will be here shortly, missus," Francie said breathlessly from the opened doorway. Then seeing the packed bags she frowned with confusion. "You're leaving? I thought you said you'd be back for supper."

Rachel forced a smile before she turned to face the girl. "Would you be a dear and carry these down for me?" She handed Francie two more coins.

"Certainly, missus." Francie struggled to keep from crying. She hated to see Mrs. Thompson leave. The woman had been so kind to her. But now at last she finally had enough to get the new shoes she so desperately needed. The blister on her foot was making it difficult to walk without pain and the scraps of paper she'd placed over the hole on the bottom of her shoe kept shredding. As soon as she could get away, she was taking herself to the mercantile store.

With a valise in each hand she carefully maneuvered down the stairs to the waiting carriage. After handing the bags over to the driver, Francie slowly climbed the steps again. Her foot was now aching something awful but she knew better than to call up to Mrs. Thompson. When the woman handed her another smaller bag and indicated she should follow her back down the steps, Francie had to grit her teeth against the throbbing pain. She needed to sit down for a while and give her foot a rest or she'd never be able to walk all the way to the store.

At the foot of the stairs, Rachel turned to the girl and gave her a huge hug. "You've been such a dear, I don't know what I'd have done without you. Thank you, sweet child."

Francie fought back tears as she watched Rachel climb into the carriage. No one ever hugged her or called her a dear child. Most of the adults she knew simply ordered her about. But Mrs. Thompson had been special. She reached down to touch the coins in her pocket. But her fingers closed over something heavy and smooth. Slowly she withdrew the rock that now rested in her pocket. What... digging deeper into her pocket she started to panic. Where was her money?

She'd counted the coins that very morning and she knew she'd placed them back in her pocket. Was there a hole? Had the coins fallen out? Frantically she pulled her pocket completely out of her skirt. There was no hole. Somehow her coins had vanished and a rock had replaced them.

"You!"

Francie jumped as a hand clamped down on her shoulder.

"You thief!" the old woman who ran the Spruce House glared at her. "She told me what you did." The woman gestured to the retreating carriage. "You cost me a good tenant and I'll not have a thief under my roof any longer. You get off my property or I'm calling the authorities and they can lock you up and throw away the key for all I care."

"But I … I didn't take anything," Francie stammered in confusion even as she looked down at the rock she still held. "Mrs. Thompson…"

"Don't even try," the woman screamed. "She told me how you tried to take her money and it's because of you she's leaving. Well that's it. Get out of here now!"

"But where should I go…" she couldn't control the shaking in her voice. "I don't know where to go…"

"Go to the devil for all I care!"

Francie backed away as the woman raised a hand to strike her. Then she turned and ran.

Dr. Grayson had the carriage stop close to the sea wall and helped Emma down.

"This isn't the spot," Emma said looking around.

"I know, but I thought we might walk a bit." Without asking he tucked her arm in his and they both stepped onto the wall. "I heard an interesting tale about the wall," he said as they slowly made their way. "You might have already heard of it." When she only shook her head he continued. "Seems a few years ago the wall was in need of repair and a young army officer by the name of Captain Dancy was put in charge. Well our young man was very taken with a local Spanish girl. I'm sorry but I don't recall her name. And since he fancied himself in love, our captain arranged for the wall to be constructed just wide enough for a couple to stroll together."

Emma smiled. "That's a lovely story."

"Well, that's not quite the end of it." The doctor grinned down at her. "Seems that Captain Dancy's love interest was from a very proper Spanish family and whenever he escorted his lady, her duenna had to accompany them. So he mistakenly thought that with the wall being only wide enough for a couple to walk abreast, the duenna would have to walk behind. But alas he didn't count on how prim the Spanish family was and when all was said and done, it was the duenna who walked with his lady and he who had to walk behind."

Now Emma chuckled. "That's a charming tale. But tell me, did it have a happy ending?"

"I'm not sure," the doctor gave her arm a pat. "But I choose to believe it did." His steps slowed. "And I think we're just about at the right spot," he said quietly.

Emma stopped. She hadn't realized how difficult it would be to return here and was more than a little grateful for the doctor's arm to steady her. Carefully she looked down at the sand then frowned.

Turning slightly she looked back at the town behind them. "You're right, this is the place, but it just looks... normal. No one passing would have any idea that a murder took place here." She shivered. "Somehow I thought it would look more sinister. I don't know what I was thinking... it's just sand, rocks and a few shells." She started to turn back but the setting sun caught on something half hidden in the sand and she paused. "Is that a bottle?" She gestured to a clump of sea grass where something reflected the sun's dying light.

"You have good eyes." Grayson released her arm and hopped down off the wall. He reached the sea grass in a few steps then carefully picked up a discarded wine bottle. After brushing away most of the sand, he handed the bottle up to Emma and vaulted back over the wall.

Emma stared at the bottle in disbelief, then looked up at the doctor. "I recognize this." Her fingers traced over the homemade design on the label. "This came from Wakefield House. James, my late husband, loved to make wine. When he passed, Gibbs took up the task."

"Would that be the wine that is served with dinner each day?"

She nodded. "Gibbs told me our last bottle had gone missing. But for it to end up here, it had to be Mr. Thompson who had taken it."

"That seems like a logical conclusion."

"But it isn't," Emma shook her head as she stared at the bottle. "According to Captain Delgado, Mr. Thompson was last seen at McConnell's Tavern and there was some type of ruckus. Why would he take a bottle of homemade wine to a tavern? It doesn't make sense."

Grayson frowned. "Well, when you put it that way …" A gust of wind blew in from the water and Emma shivered. "Let's go back before we lose the light." Taking her arm again the doctor stepped off the wall and steadied her as she stepped down. They walked quickly back to the waiting carriage.

When the carriage pulled up at Wakefield House, Emma spied Howard striding toward them.

"There you are." He helped her down. "Gibbs said you'd gone to return Thompson's possessions but he didn't think the task would take this long. We were both starting to worry."

"*You* were worried?" Emma gave him a poke in the belly with an outstretched finger. "How dare you talk about worry when you disappear for nearly two days without a word."

Howard had the good grace to actually grimace. "I guess I should have sent word. I'm sorry."

"You should be," she huffed. "And where, pray tell, have you been these last two days?"

Another gust of wind raced down the narrow street. "Let's take this inside," Grayson said, giving Howard a meaningful glance. "I'm sure Mrs. Wakefield would prefer that to standing out here."

"Good idea." Howard took Emma's arm and led her back toward the house. Gibbs, who was lighting lanterns on the veranda, paused as they arrived. "Good evening." He nodded toward the group. "Mrs. Wakefield, I've laid a fire for you in the parlor. I fear this evening has taken on a nasty chill. Would you like me to fetch you something warm to drink?"

"That would be lovely, Gibbs. Perhaps a pot of tea?"

"Coffee for me if you will," the doctor said.

"Nothing for me, Gibbs," Howard grinned. "I know where Emma keeps a bottle."

WHEN THEY WERE in her parlor with the fire starting to crackle and give off warmth, Emma cradled her cup of tea and watched Howard retrieve the bottle of bourbon he'd brought earlier. The doctor merely shook his head when Howard gestured with the bottle.

"Now can you tell me where you've been these last two days?" Emma prompted, when both men were finally seated.

"I've been at the stables."

"The stables? Whatever for?"

"You've heard about the fight at McConnell's Saturday night?" At Emma's nod, Howard continued. "Mac caught Thompson cheating at cards and that's what started the ruckus. So I followed him, Thompson that is, when he climbed out the window. But once in the alley way I lost him. I decided the man had only one choice and that was to leave town. He couldn't come back here. You suspected him of being a killer and you knew he was a thief. He had half the men in town searching for him to get their money back, so in my mind his choices were limited. I figured he'd decide his best bet was to try to hire a horse or a carriage and get out of town. And when he reached the stables, I'd be waiting for him."

"But the man never showed up," Dr. Grayson said.

"I was certain he'd show eventually," Howard continued, taking a deep drink. "But I was wrong. I didn't even know the bastard was dead until this afternoon. Did Jonathan finally get him?"

Emma exchanged a worried glance with the doctor. She knew Jonathan had been out all night by his very words. But what was she going to do if it turned out that he had caused Mr. Thompson's death?

"You suspect Jonathan Campbell?" Grayson asked.

Howard shrugged. "Only that he had it in for the man as much as I did, and since it wasn't me ..."

"Surely you can't think Jonathan would give Mr. Thompson poisoned wine," Emma said, trying to convince herself as much as them.

"Poison?" Howard exclaimed. "The rat was killed with poison?"

Grayson nodded. "I believe we might have found the source today when we revisited the spot where Thompson died."

Now Howard shook his head. "That doesn't sound right.

Campbell would use his fists on the man not resort to something as sneaky as poison. Are you sure?"

Grayson nodded again. "This is the bottle we found."

Howard stared at the bottle then looked back at Emma. "That's one of yours."

"I know," Emma started to wring her hands. "What I don't understand is that if Mr. Thompson took the bottle, who put the poison in?"

"Well you don't have to worry that anyone would think it was you," Howard said. "Anyone who knows you knows you'd never do such a thing."

Emma pressed her hand to her heart. "I never thought *I* might be considered a suspect."

"Well, it is your wine," Howard shrugged. "The label clearly proves that. And some could argue that when you discovered he'd been the one who killed Andrew, you decided to take matters into your own hands."

"That's absurd," Grayson said angrily.

"I agree," Howard continued. "But face the facts. The bottle came from Wakefield House. And if it's the most likely container for the poison, who besides Emma had access? And who would want Thompson dead?"

Emma started to shake. "I never wanted the man dead. I wanted him brought to justice."

"Then we need to figure out who *did* put the poison in this wine if indeed it was caused by the wine."

"But how can we tell?" Emma's voice trembled.

"There's a test," Grayson rubbed a hand over his face then turned to Howard, "that will detect the presence of arsenic. I'm going to speak with the authorities at my earliest opportunity tomorrow. I actually planned to tell Captain Delgado at supper this evening."

"Supper!" Emma jumped up, nearly spilling what was left of her tea. "I've completely forgotten to check." She glanced at the clock on her mantle. "What was I thinking! You must excuse me." And without a backward glance she hurried from the room.

Grayson looked back at Howard. "Surely you don't think Mrs. Wakefield had anything to do with Thompson's death."

"Of course not. Em wouldn't hurt a fly let alone kill a man no matter how angry she got." Howard downed the last of his drink. "But I think we need to find out who did as soon as possible before any suspicion falls in her direction."

CHAPTER 13

*E*mma spent another sleepless night as she struggled with the new information. Mr. Thompson had been poisoned and it was likely that the poison had been put in her missing wine bottle. But who had access and would want to see Mr. Thompson dead? And if suspicion fell on someone at Wakefield House, all her hard work at building a solid reputation for her establishment would be ruined.

She decided that she had no alternative but to take matters into her own hands. She would pay a visit to McConnell's to learn the details of what happened that night. Perhaps someone saw Mr. Thompson with the wine bottle and the poison was slipped in there.

Giving up on sleep, she rose and dressed quickly in the predawn chill. The embers in her fireplace had long grown cold but a glance at the clock told her that Sadie would already have a fire going in the bread oven. Grabbing her shawl, Emma made her way to the kitchen.

She found Sadie kneading bread dough. The scent of yeast wafted through the air. Tobias added more wood to the fire and Gibbs sat drinking his coffee. Grateful for the warmth she took a stool close to the hearth.

"I saw the light from your room," Sadie wiped her hands and reached for the tea pot. "So I set this to brew. Should be ready by now."

Accepting the offered mug Emma wrapped her hands around its warmth. "Is there anything I can do to help?"

Sadie shook her head. "I made Henny set the table last night before she left. I'm tired of her arriving late each morning and making us scramble to be ready for the first sitting."

Emma sighed. "I'll speak with her again. I'd hoped after the last talk we'd see some improvement." When Sadie only huffed, Emma hurried on. "I know she's not working out as we'd hoped, but her family is in such despair that I'd hate to let her go. And since it was Mr. Thompson who stole Auntie's cameo, he probably was the one who took the money from my office as well."

Sadie divided the mass of bread dough then placed it into two tins. She covered them both with a towel then turned back to Emma. "You've got a big heart Missus, but you can't go supporting half the town. Maybe Henny can find work doing something that she'd take a shine to."

Now it was Gibbs who harrumphed. "She's just lazy if you ask me. I've never seen a body who needs a job as bad as she does go out of their way so many times to try to lose it."

Emma set her mug down. "Then I'll have to find someone to take her place."

"Shouldn't be hard," Sadie said. "Think …"

Her word's were cut off as Willie stumbled in, dropping the load of wood he carried. "Mrs. Wakefield," he gasped, struggling for breath. "You gotta come quick! There's a dead girl by the woodshed!"

Tobias grabbed a lantern as they scrambled to follow Willie back around the kitchen to the woodpile. From the glow of the lantern Emma saw a small girl curled in a tight ball just inside the shed.

"I didn't see her at first but when I turned with the wood," Willie said, still struggling to catch his breath. "I nearly tripped over her. She's dead, isn't she!"

Emma knelt down and touched the cold flesh making the child moan. "She's not dead, just half frozen. Gibbs, give me a hand here. Tobias, go see if Dr. Grayson can come."

Gibbs gathered the child making her moan again as he lifted her into his arms.

"Come, let's get her into the kitchen where it's warm." Emma tucked her shawl around the child then followed Gibbs as he carried her. "Willie, go to the laundry and fetch the gray blanket on the top shelf and be quick about it."

When he returned Emma held the opened blanket in front of the hearth to warm it, then with Gibbs's help wrapped the child in it. She pulled Sadie's rocking chair closer to the hearth then sat with the girl in her lap. Gently she rubbed the child's back until she felt the thin body start to relax.

"Mama?" the girl's voice was a whisper as she struggled to open her eyes.

"What's going on here?"

At the sound of Dr. Grayson's voice, Emma felt the girl stiffen. "Shhhh," she said softly, "you're safe." Slowly she rocked back and forth in the chair.

"I found her at the wood shed," Willie said. "I thought she was dead but Mrs. Wakefield done brought her back to life."

Grayson squatted down in front of Emma. "Well if anyone could bring someone back from the dead it would be Mrs. Wakefield. Let's see what we have here." He rubbed his hand gently over the blanket on the child's back. "Hey, little one, you're going to be okay. Did you spend the night outside?"

Carefully he pulled part of the blanket away so he could reach her hands. "Although it was cold last night, thankfully it wasn't cold enough to cause frostbite." He pressed her hands between his warm ones. "Do you have any idea what she was doing there?" He tucked her hands back under the blanket and reached for her feet. When he touched her left foot she cried out in pain and suddenly sat up, wide eyed and terrified.

Emma ran a hand down the child's limp hair. "It's all right, you're safe here." When the girl turned to face her, Emma smiled. "I know you. You live at Spruce House." At her words the girl's eyes filled with tears. "There now, it's okay. Did you get lost last night? After we get you warm again, Tobias can take you home."

The child started to tremble uncontrollably. "I can't go back," she stammered, her voice hoarse from her ordeal. "The missus kicked me out and I didn't know where to go." Tears now streamed down her face, making tracks in the grime that covered her cheeks.

"What's going on?" The group turned as Henny stepped into the kitchen.

Sadie looked at the clock on the wall shelf. "You're late again."

Henny had the good sense to blush. "My brat of a brother turned off the alarm again. He hates when it wakes him up so early." She stepped closer. "Hey, what's she doing here?"

"She camped out in the wood shed last night," Willie said, picking up the wood he'd dropped all over the floor to stack it near the hearth.

"Well that was stupid." Henny rolled her eyes and reached for her apron on the wall peg. "It was freezing last night. I could even see my breath as I walked here this morning."

"Well now you can just walk into the dining room and get the lanterns lit for breakfast," Sadie snapped. "Willie, you go with her and get the fire going in there so folks don't catch a chill when they come down to break their fast."

Willie hurried to his task but Henny just rolled her eyes again making Emma frown.

"Sadie," the doctor said standing, "might our patient have a mug of strong tea?"

"Lots of sugar?"

"You're right as always." Taking the mug, the doctor offered it to Emma. "She'll warm up faster if we can get something hot into her. But not too much at once."

Emma held the mug to the girl's lips even as the doctor guided her small hands round the warm mug. The child sighed with the first sip. "It's so good…"

When she'd finished the mug she pulled the blanket tight about her even as she sat up straighter and realized she was sitting on Emma's lap. Tears started again. "I don't mean to be no trouble," she sniffed. "I thought I could find Henny and maybe go home with her."

"That's not going to happen," Henny said as she entered the kitchen again. "My ma would kill me if I brought her home."

"You don't have a family?" Emma asked the child.

"Her ma died years back," Henny said flatly. "They were staying at Spruce House when she keeled over dead one day. The mistress there let Francie stay on if she'd help out."

"I had a blanket on the third floor," Francie said in a whisper. "But she run me off and I couldn't get it."

"And why did she run you off?"

Francie's tears flowed faster and her breath started to hitch. "She said Mrs. Thompson called me a thief. Said I stole from her but I didn't. I swear it. I never took nothing from nobody."

"Mrs. Rachel Thompson?" Emma prompted.

Francie nodded. "She was so kind to me at first. She'd give me a coin if I fetched something for her. She even hugged me and called me a dear." Francie turned her tear streaked face to Emma. "No one ever called me a dear before. I thought she was the kindest lady I'd ever met."

"What happened to change it?" the doctor asked pulling a stool closer to sit.

Francie seemed to shrink within the blanket. "After you and Mrs. Wakefield come to bring her her dead husband's stuff, she was in a terrible rush to leave. I fetched a carriage for her then carried her bags down the stairs."

Emma felt the girl start to shiver again. "It's going to be okay, Francie. Would you like another cup of tea?"

She nodded slowly. "I ain't got no coins to pay for it though."

"Don't worry," Sadie said, fixing another mug and passing it to the doctor.

"Let the heat warm your hands," he said giving the mug back to the girl. "And drink this slowly, it's pretty hot."

"So, Mrs. Thompson was in a hurry to leave?" Emma prompted after Francie had consumed more than half the mug.

Francie nodded and looked back at Emma. "That's when she hugged me and call me 'her dear'. But after she got in the carriage I reached in my pocket and found this." She pulled out the smooth rock.

"She gave you a rock?" the doctor questioned, clearly puzzled.

"She took the coins I'd been saving and put this in their place." Francie's lip began to tremble again. "I thought she was so nice… but all the coins she'd been passing to me for running errands were gone."

"Did you tell anybody?" the doctor asked.

"I was going to tell the missus, but that's when she started screaming that I was a thief. Mrs. Thompson told her she was leaving 'cause I was a thief. Then she run me off before I could even get my blanket."

"Well you can keep this blanket," Emma said, easing the girl from her lap and into the rocking chair. "But I need to see to breakfast. You stay here and finish your tea and get warm again. Then we'll see what we can do about things."

The doctor followed Emma out as she stormed from the kitchen. "Mrs. Wakefield, are you all right?"

Emma whirled. "All right? How can anything be all right if someone can treat a child like that? First that witch Mrs. Thompson steals her money then she's run off without a care as to what might happen to her!" Emma took two steps forward and spun around again. "I'm so angry I couldn't stay in there a moment longer or I would have frightened her even more."

"Well you're doing a good job of frightening me," the doctor said calmly.

"Arrrrhhhh!" She looked up at the sky where dawn was just stating to break. "I just don't understand how someone could treat a child that way. You saw her, she's thin as a rail."

"Well, there's another problem," the doctor said. "When I was checking her feet, I found she's got a terrible sore on the bottom of her left foot. At a quick glance I'd say she had a blister that broke and she's been walking on it. If it gets infected she's going to have quite a problem."

Emma took several deep breaths to calm herself. "Is that something you can treat?"

"Certainly, but it won't be pleasant for her."

"Okay, let me get some breakfast into her first, then I'll pay you for whatever treatment you deem necessary."

Now the doctor stiffened. "Payment won't be necessary," he said flatly. "You are not the only one who cares what happens to a child like that." And with his words still hanging in the air, he turned and walked back toward his room.

Emma closed her eyes and sighed. Now she'd insulted the man. Her day had only started and already it was slowly going from bad to worse.

When breakfast was over for her guests Emma returned to the kitchen to find Henny, Willie, and Francie sitting at the worktable with plates of steaming eggs before them. From the looks of it Henny had already consumed more than half of her serving. But Francie sat on a stool with her hands folded in her lap.

"Something wrong with your food, missy?" Sadie stood on the other side of the table, her hands planted on her hips.

"No ma'am." Francie didn't look up. "It looks real nice."

"Then why aren't you eating?"

Now Francie did look up. "I know the rules."

"And just what rules might they be?"

"You don't get to eat unless you done all your chores. I ain't done any chores…"

"Well that isn't my rule," Emma said sharply making everyone jump as she entered the room.

Francie slipped from her stool and stood balancing on her good foot and the toes of her other.

Willie frowned. "Why'd you jump up like that? Mrs. Wakefield don't hit nobody."

Now Francie frowned in confusion. "You're supposed to stand if a grown-up comes into the room."

Willie looked at Emma who now stood beside Sadie on the other side of the table. "Really?"

"That's a polite thing to do." Emma gave Francie a smile and nodded as Willie slipped from his own stool to stand.

"That's stupid," Henny gave another eye roll. "You'd be jumping up all day long and never getting anything done."

"Hah, like you'd be worrying about getting things done." Sadie reached across the table and snatched Henny's empty plate. "But now that you're finished, you can start clearing in the dining room. "And you," she turned to Francie who still balanced on one foot. "you'd better sit before you fall over. Now eat them eggs before they get cold."

At Emma's nod, Francie sat back onto the stool and took a small bite of eggs. Then as if she couldn't help herself, she wolfed down the remainder on her plate.

"That was real good, Miss Sadie." Willie rose and took his plate to the wash sink. "I'll get the next load of wood now unless you want me to do something different."

"That will be fine," Emma spoke as she took a stool across from Francie. Sadie handed her another cup of tea and a plate of toasted bread. "Sadie, I think our guest could do with another serving of eggs and perhaps a biscuit." She watched Francie's eyes grow wide with surprise as Sadie set another plate in front of her.

"This is all for me?"

"And you better clean that plate," Sadie huffed, before she turned back to the stove.

"Did you get any supper last night?" Emma asked, watching the child savor each mouthful.

Francie shook her head. "The missus run me off right after Mrs. Thompson left."

"Did you have anything to eat earlier?"

Now Francie looked confused. "After morning chores I get a bowl of porridge if there's any left from breakfast. Then if I've been helpful all day the cook gives me a biscuit or two." She looked over at Sadie. "But they never tasted like this. Hers were always hard. This is so soft you don't even have to chew much."

"Francie, is what Henny said about your family true?"

Francie immediately placed her hands in her lap and looked down as her lower lip started to tremble. "My ma went to heaven when I was little."

"And you have no other family?"

She shook her head. "I ain't got no place to go. I came here 'cause I thought maybe Henny…"

"Well, don't worry about that now," Emma interrupted then rose as she saw the doctor step into the doorway. "You finish your breakfast then sit by the hearth so you can stay warm." She walked to the door and motioned for the doctor to follow her out.

"I need to apologize," she said quickly as they stepped away from the kitchen. "I didn't mean to insult you earlier. You've been nothing but kind and helpful and I…"

The doctor held up a hand to stem her words. "No, I overreacted and it's I who should apologize to you. It's just seeing a child in such distress like that…"

Now it was Emma who stopped his words by placing her hand on his arm. "Let's agree to forget it," she said giving him a smile. "I think we were both upset."

"What are you going to do?"

"I don't know. The thought of turning her over to the orphanage just doesn't sit well. She's so young and has already suffered so much." Emma blinked back tears. "She just told me they gave her a bowl of porridge in the morning and maybe a biscuit for dinner if she was helpful all day. It's no wonder she's skin and bones."

"Well, I can't help with the food, but I can fix her foot if you're willing to assist me. It's going to be painful for her but that wound has to be cleaned and treated or it's going to get infected if it isn't already."

"What's this about Willie finding a dead girl at the woodshed?"

Emma and the doctor both turned to find Aunt Daisy standing behind them, hands planted on her hips and a very annoyed expression on her face. "And why wasn't I told about this?"

"Auntie, the child wasn't... isn't dead. She's very much alive and eating breakfast in the kitchen with Sadie."

"Well, where did she come from?" Daisy demanded.

"She's been working at Spruce House but there was a ... problem," Emma hesitated. "And they let her go. She's a friend of Henny's so she came here looking for her."

"If she's a friend of Henny's then she'll be worthless. So it's no wonder they let her go. You should follow their lead and do the same for Henny. That girl is never around when you need her."

Emma blinked with surprise. She'd never heard Aunt Daisy complain about anything. Now to hear her echo Sadie....

"Well, first things first," the doctor said. "We need to see to her foot and then you can decide what should happen next."

Daisy followed Emma and the doctor back into the kitchen and stopped when she saw the child sitting at the worktable. "My word, Emma, she's just a little girl. You, child," she walked over to Francie, "how old are you?"

"I think I'm eight," Francie said hesitantly. "But I can work real hard if you'll let me stay."

"Did you have enough to eat?"

Francie nodded and smiled over at Sadie. "I ain't ever had anything that good before."

Willie came back into the kitchen with another load of

wood and Emma instructed him to fetch two pails of water and their small washtub. When the water was heated, Francie was moved to a stool closer to the hearth.

Emma watched as Doctor Grayson removed his coat and rolled up the sleeves of his shirt. She found herself staring at his bare arms as he knelt before the child. He kept a gentle chatter going, even making Francie laugh at one point as he washed her right foot and leg up to her knee. But when he gently eased her sore left foot into the warm water, she cried out.

"I know, it stings but it will be better soon. You're such a brave girl." He gently lathered soap over and around her foot and leg.

Emma moved to one side and took Francie's hand even as Daisy stepped to her other side.

"Almost done," the doctor said as he propped her injured foot on his knee and spread salve over the wound. "You've been so brave, I'm going to ask Miss Sadie if she might have a cookie or two she could give you. What do you say to that?" When he looked up at Francie, who other than her initial cry hadn't uttered a sound, he found Emma with tears streaming down her face and Aunt Daisy pressing a handkerchief to her eyes with her free hand. "Ah, maybe we should have cookies all around?"

"It feels better," Francie said slowly.

The doctor wrapped a long strip of cotton cloth around her foot. "Now I want you to be careful and try to keep this clean okay?"

Francie nodded. "Yes sir."

Daisy let go of the child's hand and reached down and picked up one of Francie's discarded shoes. "Well this is the culprit," she said, poking her finger clear though the hole in the bottom of the shoe. "No wonder she got a sore on her foot."

"This should make you feel better." Sadie set down a plate with two huge molasses cookies in Francie's lap. "Now eat up and then we'll see what else needs to be done."

Emma watched the doctor wash his hands at the sink then dry them on the towel Sadie provided. Embarrassed that he'd caught her staring as he rolled his shirt sleeves back down, Emma felt her cheeks begin to burn.

"I'll check her foot again tomorrow," he said, not bothering to hide a smile. "But I think we caught everything in time. However if she keeps wearing those shoes the problem is just going to come back."

"I have a pair of slippers I think would fit her." Daisy took the worn shoe and tried measuring it against her own foot.

Emma gave herself a shake. "Francie, I want you to stay in here with Sadie. I have some errands I need to run but when I get back we'll figure out what to do next."

"Yes. ma'am," Francie nibbled at the cookie and Emma wondered if she was trying to make the treat last as long as possible. Stepping out of the kitchen she turned as the doctor followed her out.

"You mentioned errands." He slipped his coat back on. "If you're going to be out and about, I'd recommend you get your shawl. Now that the sun is up it's certainly warmer, but the wind has a nip in it today."

"I'm going to walk down to McConnell's Tavern."

"Excuse me?"

"I'm going down to McConnell's and see if I can speak with the owner. I met Mr. McConnell once when James was alive. I doubt he'd remember me, but I'm going to see if he can tell me anything about that fight Saturday night."

"Then I'm going with you."

Emma looked up at him. "Why would you want to do that?"

Now the doctor smiled. "Because I don't want you to ruin your reputation by going into a tavern."

Emma's shoulders slumped. "I never thought of that. I've been so focused on trying to find out who put the poison in that wine bottle…"

"Then fetch your shawl and we can be off. It's a fine morning for a brisk walk."

CHAPTER 14

hen they reached McConnell's, Dr. Grayson left Emma outside and entered the tavern. The scent of stale tobacco hung heavy in the air. The main room was full of shadows as most of the window shades had been pulled to keep out the light. But the doctor could still see a man standing behind the bar polishing a set of glass mugs that rested on a tray before him.

"Morning," Grayson said moving to the bar.

"We're not open."

"I can see that. Could you tell me where I might find Mac McConnell?"

"Depends on who's asking."

"I beg your pardon. I should have introduced myself. I'm Dr. Alex Grayson. I've brought Mrs. Wakefield with me and we were hoping to speak with the owner. Could you assist me?"

Mac set down the glass and rag he'd been using and extended a hand. "Mac McConnell." He looked around. "This is my place. But you said you brought Mrs. Wakefield?"

"Yes, I convinced her to wait outside."

Now Mac rounded the counter. "Pretty little thing with reddish brown hair and big blue-green eyes?"

Grayson grinned. "That would be the one. So you do know her?"

Mac nodded. "But a lady like herself shouldn't be standing outside a place like this."

"Might you have an office we could use?"

Mac shook his head. "Wouldn't do for folks to see her coming or going even from the back door. No," he rubbed his chin. "Tell you what, there's a confection shop a block over but one. You take her there and I'll be around shortly."

"Thank you. I'll do just that."

When the doctor left the tavern he found Emma pacing back and forth on the front walk. Looking around, he was grateful to see that this end of town was still quiet.

"Couldn't you find him?" Emma challenged the moment the doctor reached her side. "Wasn't he there yet?"

The doctor took her arm and firmly turned her away from the tavern. "He was there and he's going to meet us in a few minutes."

"But why," Emma turned her head to look back as they proceeded to walk, "are we leaving?"

"Because the good Mr. McConnell was kind enough to remind me that a lady like yourself should not be seen in an establishment such as his. He's going to meet us at the confection shop."

"Oh, …" Emma stopped dragging her feet and turned back to face the way they were walking.

They had nearly reached their destination when she groaned and slowed her steps, but to no avail.

"Mrs. Wakefield, is that you?" The shrill voice belonged to Gloria Snyder, an older woman who saw herself as the town crier.

"Good morning, Mrs. Snyder." Emma had no choice but to stop.

"And who is this handsome gentleman?" the woman cooed, pointedly staring at Emma's arm the doctor had neatly trapped with his own.

Emma struggled not to sigh. "Mrs. Snyder, may I introduce Dr. Grayson. Dr. Grayson, Mrs. Snyder."

"Oh, so you're the new doctor? I hope you're not ill, Mrs. Wakefield."

"No I'm fine, thank you." Emma tried to subtly remove her arm from the doctor's but he merely tightened his hold, making it impossible for her to step aside without causing a scene.

"It's a pleasure to meet you, Mrs. Snyder," Grayson said. "What brings you out on such a fine morning?"

"Oh, I always enjoy an early promenade," she replied slyly. "One never knows who one might bump into."

"Gloria!" came an angry cry. "Are you going to stand there all day? I'm tired of waiting."

Mrs. Snyder looked back to where an elderly gentleman leaned half out of a carriage. "My husband," she said by way of explanation. "He has the patience of a gnat. But I suspect I must be getting on. It was so nice to see you out and about again Mrs. Wakefield. And Doctor Grayson, I hope to see more of you in the future." And with that she turned and made her way to the carriage. "Don't be so impatient, Horace, I'm coming. And you won't believe who I just saw…"

"Now we've done it," Emma groaned. "Gloria Snyder is one of the biggest gossips in this town."

"What's so terrible about that?" Grayson asked, as they continued down the street.

"She's going to spread the word that we were seen walking together."

They reached the confection shop and the doctor opened the door making the bell above jingle.

"And ?"

"People will draw the wrong conclusions." Grateful to find the small shop empty, Emma quickly chose a table in the corner. She sat when the doctor pulled out a chair for her.

"Would it help if I sat at a different table?"

"What?" Emma blinked, then seeing the twinkle in his eye realized he was teasing. "Oh, just sit down."

A young girl in a highly starched white apron approached their table. "What can I get for you?"

"I'd like a coffee," the doctor replied. "And the lady would like the new punch."

"No, thank you," Emma interrupted. "Just a pot of tea for me, please."

The girl hesitated. "You really ought to try the milk punch, missus. It's all the rage."

"No, thank you, but tea would be most appreciated."

"As you wish." She turned to go just as the door opened and Mac stepped inside. "Uncle Mac!"

The girl was instantly caught up in a bear hug then just as quickly set on her feet again. "You get back to work," Mac ordered. "But bring me some coffee first." Turning he walked over to the corner where Emma and the doctor sat. "My niece," he said. "My brother's oldest girl."

"She's quite lovely," Emma offered. "And I want to thank you for agreeing to meet with me."

Mac pulled out a chair and turning it around sat resting his folded arms on the back "Mrs. Wakefield, it's good to see you again. But what was so urgent that you'd come to the tavern like that? A lady like yourself should know better."

Emma blushed, then taking a deep breath she explained the situation to Mac. "So you see I'm desperate to find out who might have had access to that wine bottle."

Mac started to speak then paused as his niece served their order. When she had retreated to the back room again, he began. "So Thompson was poisoned. That certainly puts a different spin on things. Like everyone else, I believed him a victim of the fight after he was caught cheating at cards. But as far as I know, Thompson didn't have any bottle with him when he came Saturday night. He was drinking beer."

Emma frowned over her tea. "I was hoping you might have some answers. Someone must have seen Mr. Thompson with that bottle because the poison certainly wasn't in there when he took it from my house."

Mac shook his head. "Sorry I can't help you. But I have to admit I'm not sorry to see the man gone. Besides being a cheat, he was caught passing counterfeit bills."

Now Emma's head snapped up. "What? Counterfeit bills? I hadn't heard that."

"During the ruckus we had Saturday night a pitcher of beer tipped over a pile of bills still sitting on the table. And the ink on those bills ran faster than an old lady chasing her fella. I had a long talk with the local authorities Sunday morning. But that was well before we heard the bloke was dead."

"Do you think he was planning to start a ring here in the city?" Grayson asked.

"Don't know," Mac said, rubbing his chin again. "When I think back on it, the man talked a blue streak but never really said anything, if you get my drift."

"A patter to keep his mark's attention away from what he was doing?"

"Exactly." Mac beamed at the doctor as a teacher might a bright student. "So is there anything else I can help you with Mrs. Wakefield?"

"No, but I do appreciate your taking the time to speak with me." Emma offered a tired smile.

Mac rose. "You ever need to see me again, you send a runner to fetch me and I'll come straight away." He called good-bye to his niece and left the shop.

Emma stared down at her tea which had grown cold. "That was certainly kind of him. But this isn't going very well. I'm running out of ideas." Emma blinked back tears that were suddenly too close to the surface. "I know Howard didn't have anything to do with it, but Jonathan…."

"Jonathan, surely you don't mean Jonathan Campbell…." The bell over the door jingled as two ladies entered.

Emma rose. "I need to get back to Wakefield House and try to figure out what to do next." The doctor remained silent until they were back on the sidewalk. Then taking her arm he made her turn to face him.

"I want you to tell me why you believe Jonathan Campbell could be involved in this."

"I don't want to believe it of Jonathan," Emma said quietly. Then she repeated the threats Jonathan had made toward Mr. Thompson.

The doctor frowned. "That doesn't sound good. But from what I know of the man there must be another explanation."

"Somehow I have to find a way to speak with him without Clarissa knowing."

"Well, I think you're finally in luck. Isn't that Campbell coming out of the bank?"

Emma looked across the street and groaned. It was indeed Jonathan Campbell, but he was speaking with Mr. Forbes, the bank's manager. "Don't call to him," Emma said in a hushed voice as she spun around. "I don't think they've seen us."

"But I thought you wished to speak with him. This situation is perfect."

"It's not that." Emma felt her checks grow warm. "I don't

want to have to speak with Mr. Forbes." When the doctor said nothing but continued to stare down at her she gave a sigh and continued. "Mr. Forbes wants to be my financial manager. He doesn't believe a woman should be handling money, a fact that he reiterates quite frequently. And to prove his point, the last time I took in a deposit the count was off."

Now the doctor frowned. "You miscounted?"

"No," Emma sighed again. "I'd counted the deposit the evening before and prepared my tally sheet. But the next day when I took it to the bank, the count was off by a few dollars."

"Someone helped themselves to the money?"

"It certainly seems that way. At first I suspected Mr. Thompson. It started shortly after his arrival. But when I truly thought about it, that didn't make sense. The missing amounts were always small, just a dollar here or there. Never a goodly amount."

"Almost as if someone hoped you'd not notice?"

"Exactly. But it happened again yesterday and Mr. Thompson was well gone by then. So it means I have a thief in the house and the thought is less than pleasant."

"I can certainly understand that. And you can turn around now. Mr. Forbes has returned to the bank."

Emma spun around and indeed saw Jonathan crossing the street alone. Before she could decide what to do the doctor called out to him.

"Mr. Campbell, might I have a word?"

Jonathan paused and spying Emma and the doctor smiled and crossed over to their side of the street.

"Mrs. Wakefield and Dr. Grayson, you two are certainly out and about early. Most don't start their promenade until well after the noonday meal."

Emma realized that her arm was still neatly tucked within

the doctor's grasp. The gossips were going to have a field day with this, she thought.

"Jonathan, what happened the night of the fight at McConnell's?"

Jonathan blinked in surprise. "What?"

"We were wondering if you saw Mr. Thompson with a bottle of wine that night," the doctor added.

"If my memory serves me, Thompson was drinking beer," he said with a frown. "What does it matter what he was drinking? The man is dead."

"It matters because he was poisoned," Emma's words came out in a rush.

"Poisoned? No, I heard it was from a bash on the head. Who told you Thompson was poisoned?"

"I did," the doctor said simply. "The coroner will run a test but I'm positive I'm right."

"We discovered a bottle near the spot where Mr. Thompson's body was found." Emma couldn't suppress a shudder at the memory. "The doctor believes tests will prove the bottle of wine contained the poison that killed him."

"But why would you care how the man died?"

"Because the wine bottle came from my dining room." Emma almost cried the words. "Jonathan, people are going to think I had something to do with Mr. Thompson's death."

"Don't be absurd, Mrs. Wakefield. No one would think that of you."

"Is there anything you could tell us about that evening?" the doctor prompted again. "We know you didn't get home that night."

Jonathan blushed. "I hate to admit this but I really don't know much. After Mac lit the candles again and we realized that Thompson had disappeared, I left McConnell's with Thompson's brother-in-law. I believe he said his name was Smith but I wouldn't swear to it."

"Did you find Mr. Thompson?"

Jonathan shook his head. "Smith had this idea that we should wait for Thompson at Wakefield House."

"What?" Emma gasped.

"He never showed," Jonathan looked down at his feet. "We spent the rest of the night behind your woodpile waiting for him to come home but he never did. Finally at daybreak I decided that enough was enough and I left."

Emma felt her tears close to the surface again. "Jonathan, can you think of anyone who might have seen Mr. Thompson with a bottle of wine? I have to find out how the poison got in that bottle."

"I'm sorry, Mrs. Wakefield, I wish I could help you, but as I said, Thompson never went back to your house that night or Smith and I would have seen him."

"What am I going to do?" Emma said quietly after Johathan bid them good day.

"We'll go back to Wakefield House and run through the possibilities again. There has to be an explanation for this and we'll find it."

But as they made their way back, Emma's doubts grew with every step.

～

WILLIE ROUNDED the corner of the wood pile and jerked to a halt when he saw Henny perched on an upturned log. "Hey, what are you doing back here and what's that you're eating?"

Henny popped a chocolate in her mouth then tucked the box back in the deep pocket of her apron. "Never you mind."

"It's Mrs. Wakefield who's going to mind if you don't get your chores done."

Henny smiled swinging her legs back and forth. "My chores are getting done," she said with half a giggle. "I told

Francie it was her job to empty the chamber pots." Henny held her hand up to admire her fingernails. She'd helped herself to a nail chamois she'd found in one of Aunt Daisy's drawers and now her nails carried a healthy glow. "I always hated that chore." She gave a shudder. "So if I play my cards right, Francie will do it and no one will be the wiser."

"How'd you get her out of the kitchen?"

"I just waited until Sadie went out to work in the garden."

"But Mrs. Wakefield's gonna be angry when she gets back and finds out what you done."

"She'll never know as long as you keep your trap shut."

"She'll find out, believe me, and I won't even have to say nothing."

"Geez, you act like that woman walks on water."

Willie shrugged. "She's the smartest person I've ever met."

"Huh, the woman is stupid if you ask me. She doesn't even know the doctor is sweet on her."

"Don't you say that about Mrs. Wakefield," Willie took a menacing step forward. "Did you steal those chocolates? I seen a box like that in the window of Dawson's Sweet Shop but they were real costly."

"I didn't have to buy them, you fool. They were a gift."

Willie huffed. "Who'd buy a fancy box like that for you?'

Henny looked down her nose and tried to remember the look she'd been practicing in front of Aunt Daisy's mirror. "A fine gentleman gave them to me, if you must know."

Willie laughed right out loud. "You don't even know any fine gentlemen, let alone one who'd give you chocolates. So how about sharing?"

Now Henny pouted for real. "If you must know it was Mr. Thompson."

"What?"

"You heard me."

"And just why would a gent like Mr. Thompson give

chocolates to you, you being his maid and all?"

"Mr. Thompson liked me. He liked me a lot." Henny struggled against tears that threatened. "I don't know why he had to go and get himself killed. That spoiled everything."

"Well it sure did for Thompson. But what's it to you? You was just his maid."

"We were going to get married…"

"What? Are you daft? A gent like Mr. Thompson don't go around and marry his maid. Besides the man was already married. So you better get to those chores before Mrs. Wakefield gets back."

Henny sniffed. "I've got Francie doing my work. And if you run and tell Mrs. Wakefield about this, I'll tell her I caught you taking coins from her office."

"I never took no coins," Willie felt his face start to burn with anger. "I never even been in the missus' office."

"Well someone has been taking money. I heard her say something to Gibbs just the other morning."

"I wasn't even here the other morning. What are you trying to pull?"

Henny stood slowly and grinned in triumph. "I'm not pulling anything. I'm not the one who had to spend the night in jail. So you'll not talk about Francie doing my chores and I'll not tell Mrs. Wakefield I caught you taking money."

"But you'd be telling a lie."

"Hmmm, maybe, maybe not. But then who's to know it's a lie?"

"Well, when Mrs. Wakefield finds out where the poisoned wine came from you'll see how smart she is, and she'll know you're not telling the truth."

"What are you talking about?"

"She and the doctor went down to McConnell's this morning to see if that's where the wine came from. Then they'll know who killed Mr. Thompson."

"Your father killed Mr. Thompson by bashing his head in. That's why he's in jail, or have you forgotten?"

Willie shook his head. "Nope. The doctor said Mr. Thompson was poisoned, and they think it was the wine that done it."

Henny started to shake. "Mr. Thompson drank poisoned wine?"

Willie nodded. "That's what the doctor and Mrs. Wakefield are going to prove. Then you'll see how smart she is."

"But he wasn't supposed to drink the wine... she was..." Henny's voice trembled as her eyes filled with tears.

"What are you saying? Do you know something about this?"

"Mr. Thompson was going to take me away from all this..." Henny gestured toward the inn.

"Did he actually say that?" Willie challenged.

Henny stiffened. "He bought me an ice cream cone. He was always so kind to me..." her voice trailed away as a tear slid down her cheek. "When I heard Gibbs telling Sadie that his wife had shown up, I knew that would spoil all his plans. But he wasn't supposed to drink the wine... she was."

"Holy cow, did Mr. Thompson send his wife poisoned wine?" Willie scratched his head. "No, that doesn't make sense. If he knew the wine had poison then he'd never drink it." Then his eyes grew wide as he looked back at Henny. "Did you have something to do with this?"

Henny doubled over as her stomach cramped. She started to speak but when the pain hit again, she made a mad dash for the privy.

Willie stood in stunned silence. Had Henny been the one to poison the wine? He dropped the wood he'd been fetching. He had to tell Mrs. Wakefield right away. But when he turned around his heart dropped to his knees and he froze in his tracks.

CHAPTER 15

When they reached Wakefield house Emma paused at her garden gate. "I need to speak with Sadie. Why don't you wait for me in the parlor? I'll only be a moment."

Grayson nodded. "Perhaps we could have another cup of coffee?"

"I'll see to it." She couldn't help but smile as she watched him walk back toward the house.

"That's a good-looking man." Sadie joined her, carrying a basket full of flowers she'd just cut."

"Hmmm…"

"You won't find better," Sadie continued. "He's kind and talented and that's a good face to look at first thing in the morning."

Emma struggled not to blush as she felt her cheeks growing warm. "Thanks, but he's just a friend. Now, how's Francie doing?"

Sadie shrugged. "Hard to tell. Miss Daisy took her to the wash house and scrubbed her down, then found some of her own clothes for the child to wear. I left her in the kitchen but when I looked again she'd disappeared."

"What?"

"I guess we were wrong and now that the girl's got food in her belly and new clothes, she's run off."

Emma felt as if her world were crashing in around her. "Has Henny seen her?"

"That's another one that's disappeared again. I swear, Missus you've got to do something about that girl."

"You're right," Emma reached for the basket of flowers. "Let me get the doctor his coffee then I'll deal with Henny. We've her given so many chances... but you're right, this can't continue."

"Thanks be to heaven," Sadie muttered. "Did you find out anything at McConnell's?"

Emma shook her head. "Mr. McConnell was kind enough to speak with us, but Mr. Thompson was drinking beer when he was at the tavern. Somehow he managed to flee during the ruckus and no one knows where he went after that."

"Well, if the doctor is right and the wine held the poison, someone had to get to the bottle first before Thompson."

"I ..." Emma and Sadie both froze in the doorway to the kitchen. Francie sat on a high stool calmly peeling potatoes.

"What are you doing?"

Francie jumped with a start as Sadie stomped into the kitchen. "I saw these on the table with the bowl and thought you wanted them peeled. Did I do wrong?" Her lip started to tremble.

Sadie picked up one of the potatoes and noted how neatly the work had been done. "You done good, child," she said, giving Emma a look of total confusion.

Emma couldn't believe what she was seeing. Daisy had indeed given the child a good scrubbing. Her skin was no longer covered in grime and her hair, a soft shade of brown, was held in place with a ribbon.

"Francie, how is your foot?"

The girl beamed up at her. "It hardly hurts at all. And see," she pulled up her skirt and lifted her leg. "Miss Daisy let me borrow these."

Emma looked down to see that Francie was wearing a pair of Daisy's slippers. "Good, you keep them on until we can get you a proper pair of shoes." Emma watched as the girl's smile vanished and her eyes filled with tears. "But I ain't got coins no more. I was saving, truly I was, but…"

"Stop that," Emma said, more firmly than she meant to. "There will be no crying in my kitchen. If you're going to work here, I'll see that you have proper shoes to wear, is that clear?"

Francie's smile reappeared. "Then I can stay? You'll let me stay here?" At Emma's nod the girl hopped off the stool and threw her arms around Emma' waist hugging her tightly. "Thank you, thank you! I'll work hard. I promise I will."

Emma struggled to keep her own tears from falling. "That's okay." After giving the child's shoulders a gentle rub, she urged her back onto the stool. "Now, you stay in here and give Sadie a hand, all right?"

"Yes, ma'am," Francie swiped at her eyes with her sleeve. "When I finish the potatoes, I can shell the peas if you want."

Before Sadie could answer, Tobias rushed into the kitchen. "Mrs. Wakefield, thank God you're back. You gotta come quick. Frank Jefferson be here and he's trying to take Willie."

WILLIE STARED in horror at his father. "How did you get out of jail?"

"Turns out wasn't me that killed him after all. Now, you get your belongings. You're coming home with me."

"No, he's not," Emma rounded the corner and placed herself between Willie and his father.

"I ain't got no quarrel with you, Mrs. Wakefield, but that boy is coming home with me." He turned back to Willie. "I said get your belongings now."

"You mean my pouch of coins," Willie challenged. "That's what you really want. You don't care about me."

"You shut your mouth, boy, if you know what's good for you. Now get your stuff before I have to teach you a lesson."

"You're not taking that boy." Emma folded her arms over her chest. "The police released him in my custody. My custody, Mr. Jefferson. And until the police tell me differently, I'm responsible for him."

"He's my son and you'll not steal him away from me."

"He ain't going nowhere with you." Tobias, brandishing a pitchfork, moved to stand next to Emma.

"You get out of my way," Jefferson reached down and picked up a piece of wood to use as a club. "Nobody is gonna take my son away from me."

Knowing how violent his father could become and terrified that the two people he loved most in the world might be hurt, Willie took a deep breath and stepped forward. "You don't want me, like I said, you just want my money. Well you can have it, all of it, if you swear you'll leave and never bother these folks again."

Jefferson lowered the wood he'd hefted. "I could settle for that, I reckon. Though it breaks my heart you'd choose them over your own kin."

"You don't have a heart," Willie said flatly. He turned to Emma. "Mrs. Wakefield, if you'll get the pouch the police gave you, we can give the money to him and he'll leave."

Emma lifted her chin, stared at Willie and felt her own

heart swell with pride at his offer. "That's very thoughtful of you, Willie, but it's not going to happen. That money is yours and it's going to stay yours."

"He be my son so what's his is mine by law, it's only right." Jefferson's voice rose with each word. "And I'm not leaving until I have both."

"What's going on out here?"

Emma turned to see Dr. Grayson accompanied by a man she'd never seen before. Slightly taller than the doctor, he was well built with sandy colored hair. He hadn't raised his voice, but when he spoke the man radiated quiet authority.

"And who the hell are you?" Jefferson hefted the slab of wood again.

"I'm Detective Matthew Stark. And you'd be Frank Jefferson, recently released from jail, if I'm not mistaken."

Jefferson lowered the wood and licked his lips. "And what's it to you?"

"I believe you were instructed to go home and stay out of trouble when you were released. Isn't that correct?" The detective's voice was soft but held a menacing note.

"I'm just collecting my son here," Jefferson gestured to Willie. "I'll be off as soon as he gets his belongings and comes with me."

"That's not going to happen," Emma said.

"You're right. Mrs. Wakefield I presume?" Emma nodded and the detective continued. "I'm sorry Mr. Jefferson, but as Mrs. Wakefield stated, that's not going to happen. Your son was released into her custody therefore he has to stay here." As Jefferson started to interrupt, the detective simply held up a hand to stop him. "You, of course, may go and find a judge to plead your case. And if the judge agrees then the boy can be released into your custody. But until then, I believe Mrs. Wakefield has asked you to leave her property."

"This ain't right 'cause...."

Again the detective simply held up a hand. "If you refuse to leave, Mr. Jefferson, you'll give me no choice but to have you arrested again for disturbing the peace and being a public nuisance. Are you eager to go back to jail?"

Jefferson angrily tossed down the wood he held. "I'm going, but it ain't right to steal a man's son away. You ain't heard the end of this." He spit on the ground. "No, you ain't heard the end of this."

Emma breathed a sigh of relief when the man finally turned and stumbled away. "Oh, my word," She pressed a hand to her frantically beating heart.

"Might I suggest we continue this inside?" the detective said.

"A splendid idea. Mrs. Wakefield, let me assist you." This time Emma didn't object when the doctor took her arm as her legs didn't feel quite steady.

Tobias put down his pitchfork and wiped perspiration from his brow. "Sure glad I didn't have to use this." He gave Willie a wink. "And that was a mighty fine thing you tried to do, offering to give your dad your money. But son," he placed a big hand on Willie's shoulder and gave a squeeze, "don't ever let a con man like your father get the better of you. You got heart and that's for certain, but you earned those coins fair and square."

Embarrassed by his father's actions but more by the love he felt for Tobias, Willie blinked hard. "I would have if he had tried to hurt you or Mrs. Wakefield."

Tobias nodded. "Son, you mean well, but there are times when you jest got to let the adults fend for themselves. Now, what say you and I attack that old woodpile and work off some of this energy I got running through my veins?"

Inside the parlor Emma sank gratefully onto her favorite rocker.

Detective Stark stepped forward and gave a slight bow.

"Now that things are calmer, let me introduce myself formally." He pulled a slim wallet from his inside coat pocket, flipped it open, then handed it to Emma. "As I said outside, I'm Detective Matthew Stark. I'm on loan from the Jacksonville police office and I'm here to investigate the murder of Agent Langley."

Emma offered the credentials to Dr. Grayson, who closed the wallet and handed it back to the detective. "We met earlier," he said by way of explanation. "Gibbs introduced us while I was waiting for you to come in…"

"Then we heard the voices outside," the detective said, placing the wallet back in his pocket.

"Are you an…"

"An agent? No, ma'am. But I'm currently assisting with the investigation of Mr. Langley's death and matters relating to that. I understand Mr. Langley was a relative of yours?"

"My cousin."

The detective bowed again. "Then please accept my sincere condolences for your loss."

There was a light tap on the parlor door and Gibbs stepped in with the tea tray. "I hope I'm not interrupting but I thought some light refreshments might be in order."

"If there's coffee to be had, I'd truly appreciate a cup," Stark said.

"A man after my own heart." Dr. Grayson took the cart from Gibbs and pushed it farther into the room while Gibbs discreetly made his exit. He handed Emma a cup of tea then poured coffee for the detective and himself. "There's milk and sugar if you've a mind…" But the detective shook his head and took an appreciative sip.

"Good coffee."

"You must think me a terrible hostess," Emma said, "but I fear this morning has had more than its share of surprises."

"I think you are lovely," the detective said with a twinkle

in his eye, making Emma blush. "But what can you tell me about Samuel Thompson's death?"

Emma looked to the doctor then back at the detective. "We found him day before yesterday on the beach. But can I ask how you knew he had a part in Andrew's death?"

"Certainly," the detective settled back in his chair. "I've been following Thompson for several months now. He first came to the Agency's attention in Jacksonville, but he moved to Atlanta before we were positive of his identity. That's when Agent Langley was assigned to investigate. And let me say your cousin was, and still is, held in high regard within the Agency. He located the counterfeit operation in Atlanta and was instrumental in its demise. The only thing he wasn't able to accomplish was to identify the mastermind, or ringleader if you will."

"So Andrew didn't know that Mr. Thompson was involved?"

"From what I've been able to piece together, that's correct. But I'd followed Thompson's trail from Jacksonville to Atlanta. We knew the mastermind had already established counterparts in Savannah and Amelia Island. I was following your cousin to share with him my suspicions of Thompson when I heard of his murder. After speaking with the authorities in Tocoi, I was positive that Thompson was somehow involved. But tell me, how did you come to this knowledge so quickly?"

Emma set down her tea cup. "It was the cat."

"I beg your pardon?"

"One of my boarders has a cat that likes to steal socks handkerchiefs, anything that is left on the floor."

"Bandit," Dr. Grayson added with a grin. "And the name is appropriate."

"You have a cat named Bandit?" Now the detective grinned. "Please go on."

"The morning after Mr. Thompson didn't return, I went in to check his room. The cat darted in and started batting at some cords hanging from the underside of the mattress. When I investigated further, I found the cords were attached to a pouch that had been hidden under the mattress." Emma looked down at her clasped hands. "The pouch contained Andrew's watch, ring, and my Aunt's cameo brooch as well as other jewelry I couldn't identify."

"Whoa! Did you confront the man?"

"He never returned. Clarissa, that's Clarissa Campbell, Andrew's fiancé, came and after she confirmed that the jewelry was Andrew's, we called Captain Delgado from the fort. He resides here also. I knew he'd know what to do."

"I see. Well, I'm sorry I won't have the pleasure of seeing Thompson put in jail, but I can't say I'm sorry the man is dead. But who was responsible for his death? I know the authorities originally charged Jefferson. But I stopped by the jail before I came here and heard they'd already let him go."

Emma looked over at the doctor. "We're not sure who is responsible," she said finally. "That's what we were trying to discover earlier today."

Now the detective frowned. "I take it you had no luck?"

"I wouldn't exactly say that," Grayson said thoughtfully. "We were able to eliminate several who might have been involved."

The detective pulled out his notebook. "Care to share some names with me?"

Emma looked pained but taking a deep breath started. "We know my cousin Howard, Andrew's brother, spent the night in the stable."

"In the stable?" the detective looked skeptical. "Why would he do that?"

"He'd been at McConnell's the night they caught Mr. Thompson cheating at cards." The doctor picked up the story. "There was a fight of sorts and according to Mr. McConnell, the tavern owner, Thompson managed to give the men the slip. Howard told us he assumed Thompson would want to leave town as soon as possible so he waited at the stables for the man to show up requesting a horse or carriage."

"But Mr. Thompson never showed," Emma added quickly.

"Then we spoke with Jonathan Campbell, Clarissa's brother. He claims he and Thompson's brother-in-law, who was also involved in the fight, decided that they'd wait for Thompson to return here. Jonathan told us they spent the night behind the woodpile but Thompson never showed."

The detective looked up from his notes. "So where do you think Thompson went if it wasn't to return back here or to obtain a horse to leave town?"

"If my calculations are accurate, Thompson did neither of those two things because he was already dead," the doctor said.

Emma winced and Detective Stark gave her a sympathetic glance. "If this is too distressing for you, Mrs. Wakefield, I can speak with the doctor outside..."

"No, I'll be fine. It's just..."

"Mrs. Wakefield and Miss Campbell were the ones to discover Thompson's body," the doctor offered.

The detective turned back to Emma. "You have had your share of surprises haven't you."

"There's more," she took a deep breath. "Somehow after leaving the fight at McConnell's, Mr. Thompson was poisoned."

Now the detective sat back. "I heard that at the jail this morning. I stopped at the coroner's before coming here and you were right," he nodded to the doctor. "The Marsh test proved that Mr. Thompson had indeed ingested arsenic. Or rat poison, if you will."

Emma leaned forward on her chair. "What I don't understand is how the poison got into my missing wine bottle. I realize that Mr. Thompson was a thief. He had Andrew's watch and my aunt's cameo. But if he was the one who took the wine bottle from the dining room he certainly wouldn't have put poison in it."

"And it makes no sense that he'd take a bottle of wine when he was going to the tavern where he was seen consuming beer that evening," the doctor added.

"That's a puzzle all right."

"What will you do now?" Emma asked.

"Probably follow the same path you've already traveled. We've heard rumblings that Thompson was getting ready to set up a new operation here in St. Augustine. So while I'm nosing around, I'll see if I can find any leads for that avenue as well."

Emma immediately thought of the day she'd trailed after Mr. Thompson. "Ah, I don't usually follow my guests," she said hesitantly, "but I didn't understand how Mr. Thompson could claim to be a merchant and never have any samples, so... so one day when I saw him coming from the post office, I decided to follow him." Her last words came out in a rush.

Detective Stark beamed at her. "Really... do you remember where he went?"

"I followed him to the south side of town down St. George Street. I couldn't get too close so I hid behind a hawthorn bush. He greeted a man there and they both went into one of the houses."

"Could you identify the man?"

Emma shook her head. "I wasn't close enough. I can tell you the man wasn't as well dressed as Mr. Thompson but the two seemed to know each other."

"That's okay. You're quite a detective, Mrs. Wakefield. I have a map of the city in my valise. Do you think you could pinpoint the exact location of this house for me?"

"I could try," Emma hesitated. "I can give you the general location and I could see the shutters of one window had come unhinged and were propped against the house. Of course by now they might have been repaired."

Detective Stark retrieved a city map from his case and spread it out on the side table that was often used for a game of checkers. Emma leaned over the table for a closer look. "Here is the post office." She pointed with her finger. "That's where I first saw Mr. Thompson. He walked in this direction and turned here. This is where I had to stop. But the house he went to was a way down this street." She looked up. "I'm sorry but that's the best I can do."

"You've given me a place to start."

The door to the parlor flew open and Aunt Daisy breezed in. "Emma dear, whatever is going on? Dinner is ready to be served. Henny has disappeared again and Sadie is beside herself."

"Oh, dear Lord," Emma gasped, as she looked at the mantle clock in horror. "I've totally lost track of time."

"And who is this handsome gentleman?" Daisy winked moving to stand directly before the detective.

"Auntie, this is Detective Stark from Jacksonville. Detective, my aunt Miss Daisy Bennett."

"It's a pleasure." The detective took Daisy's offered hand in his.

"You must join us for dinner." Daisy beamed her most coquettish smile and turning, tucked the detective's arm around her own.

Emma passed Gibbs standing in the doorway. "I've already set an extra place next to the doctor's," he said.

"Gentlemen, you must excuse me," Emma said.

"You run along and see about dinner, dear." Daisy winked at the doctor then took his arm with her other hand. "I can manage these two handsome men by myself. And will you be staying with us, Detective?" she questioned.

"I'm hoping to do just that, Miss Bennett."

Daisy looked up at him and batted her eyelashes. "Then you must call me Aunt Daisy," she said with a flirtatious wink.

EMMA NEARLY CRASHED into Sadie carrying a tureen of venison stew as she rushed into the kitchen. "I'm sorry, I'm sorry!" She looked frantically around for what still needed to be done.

"It's okay, missus, the children helped me fine and this is the last to go in." Even as she spoke, Willie appeared, and taking the tureen from Sadie made his way back toward the dining room.

Emma collapsed on a stool and pressed a hand to her beating heart. "I'm so sorry. I can't believe that dinner completely slipped my mind."

Sadie shook her head. "It's not like you don't have more important things to worry with right now."

"Gibbs said that Henny has disappeared again?"

Now Sadie frowned as she set a cup of tea in front of Emma. "I figured you done let her go."

"No, I haven't seen her since we got back from McConnell's." Emma took a grateful sip of the steaming liquid. "What with Willie's father showing up that way..."

Gibbs entered the kitchen followed by Willie and Francie. "Dinner is a success," he stated proudly. "Complements on the chicken and dumplings, Sadie. Captain Delgado said to tell you that along with the gopher-tortoise stew, your chicken and dumplings is his favorite."

"Good when a man knows what he likes," Sadie nodded. "Now let's get these pots washed then we'll enjoy our own dinner."

Francie stared in wonder at the food spread out before her. "All this," she looked up at Emma. "This is more than Christmas!"

"That's cause Miss Sadie is the best cook in all of St. Augustine," Willie said with a mouth full of stew."

Francie took a delicate bite and sighed. "I ain't never tasted nothing so good. But where is Henny? Ain't she coming to dinner?"

~

WHEN THE MEAL WAS COMPLETED, Emma rejoined Dr. Grayson and Detective Stark in her private parlor. Aunt Daisy had abandoned the detective in favor of the Acosta's baby, so the gentlemen each enjoyed a glass of port and Emma decided she deserved a glass of wine as well.

"I don't think I've ever had someone old enough to be my grandmother flirt with me before." Detective Shark gazed down at his port.

Emma started to choke on her wine but the doctor merely laughed and gave her a hearty pat on the back. "I hope she didn't embarrass you," Emma said when she finally caught her breath. "She means no harm."

"Actually it was quite delightful." Stark grinned. "But I did want to ask you about accommodations here, if you have the room."

"We do. Do you have a length of stay in mind?"

"I'm going to have to play it by ear if that's possible. I'll need to stay until I can find out who is responsible for Thompson's death and then if Thompson was successful getting another counterfeit ring up and running. Your information about where he went that day, Mrs. Wakefield, will be most helpful in that regard."

"When you finish your port, I can show you to your room if you wish. It's actually next door to the good doctor."

"And I can personally vouch for the food," Grayson patted his flat stomach. "Don't know when I've ever eaten so well."

"If dinner today was an example of the fare you serve, you'll have no complaints from me. And..."

The detective's words were cut off as the door to the parlor flew open and Sadie rushed in with Willie in tow. "Excuse me, ma'am, but the lad has some information that you and the detective need to hear."

Willie shifted nervously from foot to foot. Sadie gave his shoulder a cuff and he caught his breath. "It's about Henny, Mrs. Wakefield."

Emma groaned. "Did you find her? What has she done now?"

"We was talking behind the woodpile... before my father showed up. She was eating chocolates that she said Mr. Thompson give her."

Emma looked at Dr. Grayson. "Well now we know where the missing chocolates ended up."

"Care to explain?" Stark asked.

"Yesterday I assisted Mrs. Wakefield when she returned Mr. Thompson's clothing to his wife." Dr. Grayson set down his port. "The woman was staying at Spruce House at the time. She seemed unusually upset that a box of chocolates that she'd sent to him was not included with his possessions."

"It's curious, isn't it," Emma said frowning in thought. "She didn't seem to care about his clothing, even left some of it on the ground after searching though his valise. But she was desperate to find the chocolates. Then right before she took her leave she told the owner that Francie stole things from her so Francie got run off."

"Who is Francie?" The detective rubbed his hand over his face. "I'm having a hard time keeping up."

"Francie was working at Spruce House when Mrs. Thompson was staying there. Evidently Francie ran errands for her. I'm sure Gibbs told me she was the one who brought the candy for Mr. Thompson."

"But why would his wife be concerned about a box of chocolates? Seems to me that after learning her husband was dead she'd have more important things to worry about."

"Do you think she was involved in his ah... other business?" Grayson asked.

"That's a good question. But you say she left yesterday?"

Emma nodded then turned back to Willie. "Where is Henny now?"

"I don't know, ma'am. But that's not all. When Henny found out Mr. Thompson had been poisoned, she started talking all crazy like. She kept saying how it was his wife that was supposed to drink the wine, not him."

"What?" All three adults spoke at once.

"Henny said Mrs. Thompson was supposed to drink the wine?" Emma couldn't believe what she was hearing.

Willie nodded. "That's what she said. She said Mr. Thompson wanted to marry her but he couldn't 'cause he was already married. Like I said, she started talking real crazy. I would have told you this right off but then my father showed up and it went right out of my head."

Emma looked at Sadie. "Do you know where Henny is?"

Sadie shook her head. "I've asked Gibbs and Tobias to start looking for her."

At that moment a solemn faced Gibbs stepped into the parlor doorway. "I've found the girl but I'm afraid we're too late."

The group followed Gibbs to the back of the woodpile. Tobias was just pulling an old sheet over the body on the ground while Francie stood off to the side with tears running down her cheeks.

"Oh dear God," Emma gasped. "What happened?"

"Looks like she just fell over dead," Tobias said rising. "Didn't see any wounds."

The doctor moved to kneel beside the body and gently pulled back the sheet to expose Henny's face.

Francie's sob broke the silence and Willie stepped closer to her. "I'm sorry that she's dead, but you don't need to cry about it."

"She was my friend," Francie hiccuped.

"She wasn't a very good one if you ask me," Willie said. "She made you clean the chamber pots."

"But she was my only friend. Now I don't got any."

"Awww," Willie sighed and placed an arm around Francie's trembling shoulders. "I can be your friend if ya want." But he stiffened as Francie suddenly turned and threw her arms around his waist and cried hard enough to wet his shirt. Not knowing what else to do he patted her back and sent Sadie a "help me out here" look over Francie's shoulders.

Feeling her admiration for Willie grow, Emma stepped over and gently pulled Francie away. "Come on, little one, you don't need to be out here. Sadie, would you take Francie back to the kitchen?"

Sadie gathered the girl in her arms and hugged her close. "You got friends here, child. You gonna have more friends than you can count. Now what's all this about you doing chamber pots...." And with that, the two made their way back to the kitchen.

Dr. Grayson shifted the sheet to cover Henny's face again then rose. "Tobias was right there aren't any outward signs of trauma so she wasn't shot or cut. But I'm concerned." He held up a decorated box lid. "Where did this come from?"

"That's the top of the chocolate box." Willie stepped

forward, careful to keep his eyes from straying to the body on the ground. "Like I said, Henny was eating them and I saw her put that lid on the box before she shoved it into the pocket of her apron."

The doctor nodded. "We need to find the rest of that box."

"It's here," Tobias walked toward the back of the wood-pile. "I seen it when I was looking for her." He reached between two splits and withdrew an empty box.

Dr. Grayson placed the lid back on the box. "Tobias, will you fetch the wagon?" He turned to Emma. I'm going to take this," he indicated the empty box. "Tobias and I will take Henny to the coroner to get some answers, then we'll need to notify her family."

Emma pressed a hand to her heart. "They are going to be devastated. How do you tell a parent that their healthy child is dead?"

"I'd suggest we wait until we have some answers to give them," Grayson said quietly as Tobias rounded the corner with the wagon.

"Let me give you a hand." The detective stepped forward and together the two men gently lifted the lifeless body into the bed of the wagon. "Do you want me to accompany you?" he asked, as the doctor arranged the sheet more securely around the body.

"No, but thanks. Why don't you stay here and get settled in. Mrs. Wakefield, if you feel you need to be the one to notify her family I'll come back and fetch you after we know why she died." Grayson watched the last of the color drain from Emma's cheeks. "Will you be all right?"

Emma gave herself a shake. "I'm fine. This is just such a shock…"

Catching the doctor's look, Detective Stark stepped forward and offered his arm to Emma. "Mrs. Wakefield, I'd truly appreciate being shown to my room." Not giving her a choice, the detective tucked Emma's arm within his own and turned toward the house. "Willie," he called over his shoulder, "would you ask Miss Sadie to make Mrs. Wakefield some strong tea?"

"I can do that," and darting around the couple, Willie sprang toward the kitchen.

≈

EMMA PACED from one end of the parlor and back as Gibbs lit the evening candles. "I should have gone with them," she said yet again. "What could be taking so long?"

Detective Stark sat with his legs stretched out as he cradled a glass of whiskey. "When the cause of death isn't apparent it can take some time to find the answers."

"I know that," Emma struggled not to snap. "But I should have gone with them."

"Mrs. Wakefield, please, you're exhausting me watching you walk back and forth like this. Now sit down and be reasonable."

Emma flopped down on her rocker with a huff.

"You don't have any medical experience so you wouldn't be any help at this point." Stark continued. "I'm sure the doctor knows what he is about, so just be patient and hopefully he'll be able to supply some answers...soon."

"But I should..." Emma's words broke off as the door to the parlor opened and the doctor hurried in. "Where is Willie?" he demanded. "I need to see him right away."

"I'll fetch him," Gibbs said, alarmed by the doctor's tone.

"And Francie," the doctor called, "fetch her also."

"What's going on?" Detective Stark rose from his chair. "Were you able to determine how the girl died?"

Dr. Grayson nodded. "She was poisoned."

"What?" Emma, who had also jumped to her feet as the

doctor entered, sat back down on the rocker as if her legs would no longer support her.

"On a hunch I asked the coroner to run the Marsh test on the empty chocolate box and it tested positive for arsenic."

"So the girl ate poisoned chocolates?" the detective asked.

Grayson nodded. "She died as Thompson did: from arsenic poisoning."

"I don't understand any of this." Emma stood again as Gibbs entered with Willie and Francie, followed by both Tobias and Sadie.

"Now what's going on?" Sadie demanded. "We're serving supper in less than an hour and I've got a beef cake in the oven."

"Are we in trouble?" Willie struggled to keep his voice from shaking. Something awful was happening and since Henny had died all he could think of was that Mrs. Wakefield was going to send him back to his father.

"You're not in trouble," Emma said quietly.

The doctor turned to Willie. "Did you eat any of the chocolates Henny had?"

"No sir," Willie said in a halting voice.

"Son, it's important that you tell me the truth."

"No, sir," Willie said more forcefully. "I asked her to give me a piece, but she wouldn't share."

"You're sure?"

Willie nodded. "Did Henny steal the chocolates after all?"

"Henny wouldn't steal," Francie interrupted. "Henny was kind. She wouldn't steal no chocolates cause she wasn't a thief. That man who said he was Mr. Thompson was the thief."

Emma reached out and laid her hand on Francie's shoulder. "Francie, what do you know about Mr. Thompson?"

"He come to see the missus but she was out with her pa. He told me to let him into her room to wait for her so I did.

Then I went back to my pallet at the end of the hall. But he didn't wait. I seen him when he left and he had the missus' bottle of wine. The one Henny sent over as a gift for her. Like I said, Henny was kind."

"I see," Emma nodded. "Sadie you can take the children back to the kitchen. I'll be in to help you shortly."

Emma waited until Francie and Willie were out of earshot. "Henny had to be the one who put the poison in the wine. But where would she have gotten arsenic?"

"I can answer that," Tobias shuffled from foot to foot. "We keeps rat poison in the tool shed. I keeps it up on the top shelf. Few days ago I found it in a different place. I didn't think much of it till this minute. But that's when I seen Henny coming out of the shed. She told me she'd been looking for Willie and… and I jest didn't think nothing of it at the time."

The doctor nodded. "That could explain a lot. And Mrs. Wakefield, didn't you tell me just this morning that money was missing from your office again? A small amount I think you said."

"Yes but…"

"Could you tell me the exact amount?"

Emma straightened. "Of course, it was sixty-five cents."

"Sixty-five cents," the doctor said at the same time as Emma.

"But how…"

She watched him reach into his pocket and withdraw a small handful of change and a delicate cameo. "Sixty-five cents." He offered the coins. "Henny had these in her apron pocket along with this scarf and cameo. He withdrew a long gray-blue silk scarf from his other pocket. "I took the liberty of notifying Henny's parents and they've stated this wasn't hers."

"That's Aunt Daisy's missing cameo." Emma shook her

head as she reached for the scarf. "So Henny was the thief after all."

"But if Henny poisoned the wine in the hopes of getting rid of Thompson's wife," Detective Stark said, "am I to understand Thompson drank the wine meant for his wife?"

Grayson nodded. "What I don't understand is why Thompson would give Henny poisoned candy."

"Because he didn't give it to her," Emma rubbed at the growing ache in her forehead. "Just as Mr. Thompson took the wine meant for his wife, Henny stole the candy meant for Mr. Thompson."

"But she told Willie that Thompson gave it to her."

"He couldn't have." Emma took a deep breath and tried to make her thoughts align. "The morning after Mr. Thompson didn't show for breakfast, I checked his room. That's when I found Andrew's jewelry. The candy was on the dresser with a note stating it was from his wife and telling Mr. Thompson where she was staying. I simply assumed he had gone to spend the night with his wife."

"Okay…"

"But Mr. Thompson never came back to his room," Emma continued. "That afternoon was when Clarissa and I found his body. Mr. Thompson was already dead. He couldn't have given Henny the candy."

"So Henny helped herself to the candy not knowing Thompson's wife had poisoned it?" Stark questioned.

"That would explain why Mrs. Thompson was so desperate to find the box yesterday…" the doctor said.

Emma nodded. "This is finally starting to make sense." She looked at Detective Stark who still wore a confused expression. "Rachel Thompson sent her husband poisoned candy. Then when she found out he'd died not from the fight as we all originally thought, but from poison, she was desperate to retrieve the candy box that could lead us back to her."

"But when the box wasn't there," the doctor picked up the story, "she realized that since Francie had been the one to deliver the chocolates, the girl would be able to identify her as the source of the gift."

"She labeled Francie a thief so the old woman who manages Spruce House would run the child off, then Rachel Thompson made her escape," Emma finished.

"Okay that makes sense," the detective said. "But what I still don't understand is why she'd send her husband poisoned chocolates in the first place. She had to know what the results would be if he ate them."

"Not necessarily," Dr. Grayson moved to the sideboard and poured himself a drink. "If Thompson ate just a piece or two he'd probably have some very unpleasant stomach issues. My guess is that Henny died from consuming the entire box herself."

Emma sat on the edge of the sofa, suddenly exhausted. "What a tangled web. Mr. Thompson kills Andrew because of the counterfeit operation, then is kind to Henny so she thinks he has designs on her. She sends poisoned wine to get rid of his wife, but Mr. Thompson steals the wine and dies. Mrs. Thompson sends her husband poisoned candy which Henny steals and consumes causing her death. This is all such a waste."

"Will you go after Mrs. Thompson?" Dr. Grayson asked.

"I'll certainly pass the information to my superiors. But right now I doubt they'll want to pursue the matter. I was sent to investigate Andrew Langley's murder and thanks to both of you I can report who killed him and that his killer is no more. The second part of my assignment was to be sure Thompson hadn't started another counterfeit ring. And I'll be looking into that tomorrow. But for tonight, I'm thinking a good supper and a decent night's sleep will be just the ticket."

Emma rose and headed for the door to see about supper. "That sounds like a wonderful plan all around."

∼

WHEN THE EVENING meal was over Emma shared the last few details with Aunt Daisy, Gibbs, Sadie and Tobias.

"If Henny hadn't taken that chocolate she'd still be alive," Tobias said sadly.

"Well, I might have wanted her gone," Sadie twisted her dish cloth, "but I didn't mean for her to die."

Daisy ran the missing silk scarf slowly between her fingers. "You know, if she had asked me, I would have given her this. There was no need to take it."

Gibbs set down his coffee cup and rose. "The girl was a thief and she brought about her own demise. My suggestion is that we each put this from our minds and get a good night's rest. I'm sure things will be brighter on the morrow. And I for one will be happy to put all this drama behind."

"Speaking of sleep, Emma dear," Daisy said as the others began to leave the kitchen. "I've had Tobias help me set up a pallet for Francie in my room."

"You want the child to sleep with you?"

Daisy nodded. "She'll be no problem and I've plenty of room. You don't object, do you?"

Emma leaned over and kissed her aunt's cheek. "I love you, Auntie. You have a heart of gold."

Daisy smiled and returned Emma's embrace. "Sometimes, Emma, we get what we want most in life but it doesn't come in a traditional package."

Emma slowly made her way to her room, Daisy's words going round and round in her mind. Pausing on the balcony outside her door, she looked up at the stars. The night air was crisp and carried the faint scent of wood smoke. She pulled her shawl more tightly about her shoulders and knew she'd appreciate the fire Gibbs would have already started in her room. Tonight the full moon was fading, casting the scene below in darkening shadows. But the sky was clear and the stars so bright. And as always, at times like this her thoughts turned to James.

They had always talked of children, of having a big family. But James was gone and with him her dreams had died. Yet today, she realized she'd all but inherited two children. Willie was going to stay with them even if she had to take his father to court to make it legal, she decided. And little Francie deserved so much better.

Not a traditional package, she thought again. She blew a kiss to the stars in thanks. "I'll do my best," she whispered to the night. "I'll make Wakefield House a success for all of us. We are a family, just not in a traditional package."

AUTHOR'S NOTE

St. Augustine holds the distinction of being our country's oldest city. Our tale begins in 1880 when tourists from the north were just discovering this quiet retreat which offered a respite from harsh winters.

Traveling to St. Augustine was not always easy. Today, that sixteen mile trip from Tocoi to St. Augustine, would be about a twenty-six minute drive. In 1880, it was a bumpy and uncomfortable four hour jaunt.

Emma Wakefield's boarding house was modeled after the Ximenez-Fatio House located on Aviles Street. Built in 1798, as a family home, the house eventually became known as Miss Fatio's and was considered St. Augustine's most fashionable boarding house. Beautiful pictures of the building and layout can be found at XimenezFatioHouse.org. Tours are offered daily.

Gopher-tortoise stew was indeed considered a favorite dish by the guests at Miss Fatio's.

Winslow's Soothing Syrup (mentioned for Mrs. Acosta's teething baby) contained morphine, cannabis, heroin, and powdered opium. It was finally taken off the market in 1938.

The Secret Service was established on April 4, 1865, by President Lincoln to prevent the illegal production or counterfeiting of money. It was estimated that at that time, a third of the nation's money was counterfeit. The Service's first chief, William Wood, was successful in closing more than 200 counterfeiting plants in his first year.

In 1901, after Presidents James Garfield and William McKinley had been assassinated the Secret Service took on the responsibility of guarding the President.

Liberties taken:

The official police department in St. Augustine would not be established for another five years.

The *St. Augustine Gazette* was created for the story.

The *Ladies' Home Journal* is an American magazine, first published on February 16, 1883.

Sadie's Ginger Cake

4 ounces unsalted butter
4 ounces dark brown sugar (soft)
3 eggs, beaten
8 ounces black treacle *
8 ounces flour
2 tablespoons ground ginger
1 teaspoon ground allspice
1/2 teaspoon salt
1 tablespoon bicarbonate of soda

Whip the butter and brown sugar until fluffy. Beat in the eggs one at a time. Add the treacle and mix well.

Sift flour two times adding the allspice, salt, ginger, and bicarbonate of soda.

Gently fold the dry mixture into the wet.

Pour the batter into a prepared tin and bake for 50 to 60 minutes in a slow oven (325) or until top springs back when pressed.

Cool in its tin. Can be stored for a few days.

* molasses may be substituted

ACKNOWLEDGMENTS

A sincere thanks to the many folks who helped make this work possible:

To friends Barbara Cordes, Colleen Ezzell, Janet Kuchler, Linda Lark and Bernice Picard, - whose insights and enthusiasm proved invaluable.

To St. Augustine Historical Society - an ever flowing font of knowledge.

To the guides at the Ximenez-Fatio House - to whom the residents of Wakefield House owe a great deal indeed.

To Dar Albert - our talented and ever patient cover artist at WickedSmartDesigns.com